If the walls of Stockwell Mansion could talk...

...we'd spill our guts—no matter how ferociously "Big Daddy" Caine Stockwell blustered! You *must* remember his little conscience-cleanser—where he let slip that his wife may *not* have drowned all those years ago after all...! Understandably, his children have launched a full-fledged search for their mother. So far, their devoted efforts have unearthed divorce papers dated six months *after* Madelyn's supposed death, confirming that Caine's sickbed ramblings are tinged with truth. Well, we've seen a certain out-of-town address where secret bundles of cash are mailed each month—let's just say the Stockwells are hot on Mumsy's trail....

Speaking of *hot*, we've fixed our attention on family darling Kate Stockwell and her former flame, Brett Larson. Their engagement crumbled years ago, but the chemistry between them has *never* stopped simmering. Now he's a crackerjack investigator determined to find the elusive Madelyn. But his plan requires that Kate act the part of *Mrs.* Larson. Will the "princess" agree to the scheme? Heck, yes—and in less time than it takes to say "I do!"

Mercenary Jack Stockwell wrangles with a lovely mother of two in *The Millionaire and the Mom*, SE #1387, by Patricia Kay, available April 2001 only from Silhouette Special Edition.

Dear Reader,

While every romance holds the promise of sweeping readers away with a rugged alpha male or a charismatic cowboy, this month we want to take a closer look at the women who fall in love with our favorite heroes.

"Heroines need to be strong," says Sherryl Woods, author of more than fifty novels. "Readers look for a woman who can stand up to the hero—and stand up to life." Sherryl's book *A Love Beyond Words* features a special heroine who lost her hearing but became stronger because of it. "A heroine needs to triumph over fear or adversity."

Kate Stockwell faces the fear of knowing she cannot bear her own child in Allison Leigh's *Her Unforgettable Fiancé,* the next installment in the STOCKWELLS OF TEXAS miniseries. And an accident forces Josie Scott, Susan Mallery's LONE STAR CANYON heroine in *Wife in Disguise,* to take stock of her life and find a second chance....

In Peggy Webb's *Standing Bear's Surrender,* Sarah Sloan must choose between loyalty and true love! In *Separate Bedrooms...?* by Carole Halston, Cara LaCroix is faced with fulfilling her grandmother's final wish—marriage! And Kirsten Laurence needs the help of the man who broke her heart years ago in Laurie Campbell's *Home at Last.*

"A heroine is a real role model," Sherryl says. And in Special Edition, we aim for every heroine to be a woman we can all admire. Here's to strong women and many more emotionally satisfying reads from Silhouette Special Edition!

Karen Taylor Richman
Senior Editor

Please address questions and book requests to:
Silhouette Reader Service
U.S.: 3010 Walden Ave., P.O. Box 1325, Buffalo, NY 14269
Canadian: P.O. Box 609, Fort Erie, Ont. L2A 5X3

Her Unforgettable Fiancé

ALLISON LEIGH

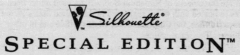

SPECIAL EDITION™

Published by Silhouette Books

America's Publisher of Contemporary Romance

Special thanks and acknowledgment are given to Allison Leigh for her contribution to the STOCKWELLS OF TEXAS series.

For all who have been blessed with true love, and for all who are still searching.

 SILHOUETTE BOOKS

ISBN 0-373-24381-2

HER UNFORGETTABLE FIANCÉ

Visit Silhouette at www.eHarlequin.com

Printed in U.S.A.

Books by Allison Leigh

Silhouette Special Edition

Stay... #1170
The Rancher and the Redhead #1212
A Wedding for Maggie #1241
A Child for Christmas #1290
Millionaire's Instant Baby #1312
Married to a Stranger #1336
Mother in a Moment #1367
Her Unforgettable Fiancé #1381

*Men of the Double-C Ranch

ALLISON LEIGH

started her career early by writing a Halloween play that her grade-school class performed for her school. Since then, though her tastes have changed, her love for reading has not. And her writing appetite simply grows more voracious by the day.

She has been a finalist for the RITA Award and the Holt Medallion. But the true highlights of her day as a writer are when she receives word from readers that they laughed, cried or lost a night of sleep reading one of her books.

Born in Southern California, Allison has lived in several different cities in four different states. She has been, at one time or another, a cosmetologist, a computer programmer and a secretary. She has recently begun writing full-time after spending nearly a decade as an administrative assistant for a busy neighborhood church, and currently makes her home in Arizona with her family. She loves to hear from her readers, who can write to her at P.O. Box 40772, Mesa, AZ 85274-0772.

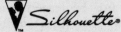

Chapter One

He's here.

That was Kate Stockwell's first thought when she heard the faint sound of the door closing to the entry of Stockwell Mansion.

God help me.

That was Kate Stockwell's second thought.

She drew in a long breath and slowly set the cordless phone that she'd been clutching with a white-knuckled grip on the nightstand. She stared blindly at the full-length mirror lining one wall of her spacious bedroom suite. The fact that her breath was unsteady was something she chose to blame on the phone conversation she'd just had.

It certainly couldn't be because of *him*.

"Kate!" The yell drifted up the stairs and along the spacious hallway to her bedroom. That was Cord. Blunt, straightforward Cord. Cord's twin, Rafe, would never bellow that way. He was too controlled. And Jack, well, her third and oldest brother simply didn't raise his voice to Kate. Ever.

"Hustle it up!" Cord yelled again.

Kate sighed and looked at her reflection again. Really looked. Her ice-blue silk suit screamed "Woman Power." Unfortunately, as she smoothed her hand down the perfectly tailored jacket, her hand trembled. Badly.

She touched a finger to the corner of her lips that she'd already glossed carefully with a pinkish hue. Her hair gleamed, grazing just below the shoulders of her suit, adding just the right touch of casual.

She knew she was taking too long. They were waiting for her. But *he* would be with them.

Kate swallowed, needlessly adjusting the drape of her delicate, silver necklace. She jiggled her knees in the narrow silk slacks, making sure the fabric fell just so.

What was she doing?

Her clothes were fine. Her makeup was fine. Even the matching pale blue lace bra and panties that she wore beneath the jacket and slacks were fine.

Gracious. Was anything more pathetic than a mature, thirty-year-old woman dithering over her appearance just because she had to go down to a room filled with her dominating big brothers…and an old lover?

Not just an old lover, her mind whispered.

Him. Brett Larson.

It wasn't like it was the first time she'd seen him recently, either. It seemed that every time she turned around, he was at the house for one reason or another. To go over some detail with Cord or Rafe. So it wasn't as if she was bracing herself for that first shock of seeing him after eight years.

Eight long years, her mind whispered.

She frowned. "Hush up." The only reason she was so uneasy was that phone call.

The excuse didn't convince her any more this time around than it did the first time. Yes, she was upset about the young patient who'd just been yanked from her program. But the true culprit was *him*.

She straightened her shoulders, dashed her fingers through the freshly cut and styled ends of her hair and strode out of her bedroom.

She was a Stockwell. Dealing with life's curveballs was part and parcel of her existence.

So why did she feel as if every nerve inside her was frayed to the point of unraveling?

She could hear them talking before she entered the study and a fresh wave of nerves rippled uneasily down her spine.

Oh, really. Why was she torturing herself like this? She didn't *have* to go in there. Didn't have to put herself in this position where she felt awkward and useless and—

"Kate." Jack spotted her hovering like a ninny outside the doorway and his lips stretched into a rare smile.

No escape, now. She focused on Jack—avoiding Brett—and walked into the room, going straight to him for a hug. "So, my favorite world traveler has returned yet again," she said in a voice that was a little too husky.

Jack wrapped his strong arms around her, lifting her right off her feet and she swallowed hard, clinging a little too fervently. And realizing it, she pressed a smacking kiss lightheartedly to his hard cheek as he set her back on her feet.

He was big and broad and so dear to her. She loved all three of her brothers, but Cord and Rafe were twins and they shared a special closeness. It was Jack who'd been Kate's rock when she'd needed him. After her breakup with—

"Hello, Kate."

Jack gave her an imperceptible nudge of encouragement, and she swallowed past the growing knot that seemed determined to strangle her. Then she turned to face the other man.

Him. Her ex-fiancé.

"Brett," she greeted smoothly. "How are you today?" Polite, meaningless words said across a bookcase-filled room to a tall, brown-eyed man whom she'd once thought she'd known as well as the back of her hand.

Now, after all these years, he was just a stranger.

A six-foot-three-inch stranger, with thick, dark messy waves that her traitorous fingers still remembered stroking back from his hard, long face, away from his chocolate-brown eyes as he leaned over her....

"Fine," the "stranger" replied, a little twist to his lips. "You?"

That chocolate gaze was anything but melting and warm now, Kate noticed, and told herself she was glad.

"Touching as this is," Rafe drawled, saving her from answering. "Why don't we get down to business?"

"Yes," Cord agreed. "I left Hannah with Becky waiting at the pediatrician's office and I want to get back to them."

Kate held her breath, embarrassingly grateful when Brett finally looked away from her, to focus on the others. She wished Hannah was here. The woman who'd become Kate's friend, then Cord's wife, after she'd brought sweet little Becky into the Stockwell home, would have provided some badly needed moral support.

"Guess that means I'm on," Jack was saying, and Kate realized she'd been staring at Brett's back. She mentally shook herself and focused on her brother. He'd propped a flat wrapped parcel across the arms of a wing chair and was peeling away the brown paper to reveal the whirls and curls of a fussy, gilded frame and the corner of a painting.

"I found this in France," he said as he tore away the rest of the paper and let it drift to the floor beside his feet. He pointed at the artist's signature in the lower corner. "Painted by Madelyn LeClaire."

But Kate wasn't looking at the signature. She stared at the portrait, feeling as if all the oxygen in the room had disappeared.

"Good Lord," Rafe finally breathed, breaking the shocked silence that had filled the room.

"It looks just like Kate did when she was a girl," Cord murmured.

"Yup." Jack looked at the painting along with the rest of them, as if even he couldn't believe it. And he'd been the one to find it. He'd been the one to call the rest of the family from France and tell them he'd picked up the trail of Madelyn's from France to New England and that he was bringing back something astonishing that they all had to see. "I about fell over when I saw it."

"You think we ought to take it to the old man's room and show it to him?" Rafe didn't look particularly enthusiastic about his suggestion.

"Shove it in Dad's face as proof of the lie he raised us to believe?" Cord grimaced. "He's so doped on pain meds for the cancer, it wouldn't faze him."

"Even if he is coherent, it wouldn't faze him," Jack

murmured without emotion. His blue gaze settled on Kate. "Feel like you're looking in a mirror, kiddo?"

She heard the words through a fog. "How—" Words wouldn't come. She shook her head.

Jack seemed to understand, though. "It was hanging in a tiny art gallery outside of Paris. Cost a fair piece, too." He stepped away from the painting, allowing room for his siblings to move in for a closer look.

Standing behind them, Kate listened to her brothers go off on the outrageous price of art until she wanted to scream. Then Brett slowly turned his head, his gaze pinning hers.

It was too much. Her eyes suddenly burned and she turned away, walking hurriedly out of the study.

Madelyn LeClaire had painted that portrait that uncannily resembled Kate.

Madelyn LeClaire…aka Madelyn Johnson Stockwell. Her mother.

Her mother who had supposedly died in a boating accident years ago.

Her father, Caine, who lay bedridden in his room in this very house had told them so. Until a few months earlier when, apparently in some attempt at cleansing his conscience that had to be weighted down with a lifetime of sins, he'd divulged that Madelyn may still be alive. And that, when she'd left her home and her children still in it, she'd been pregnant with another man's child.

Since that moment, Kate's brothers had been turning over heaven and earth trying to find out if it were true. And where she was now.

Had Madelyn had another daughter? A daughter who was the true subject of that painting? It made sense, considering Caine's claim of her pregnancy, but so much of what Caine said these days was pure delusion.

Kate walked blindly through the house, her arms clasped around her body as if to hold her shakiness at bay. Well, she could keep the shakes at bay, but the tears flooding her eyes were another matter.

"Kate. Are you all right?"

She stiffened. Oh God. Why did *he* have to follow her? She swiped her fingers across her cheeks and dashed her hair away from her face, realizing she'd wandered into the sunroom. "Of course," she answered airily. "Why wouldn't I be?"

She reached out to adjust the angle of a small fern, but her shaking hands knocked it askew and it tumbled from its narrow perch, sending rich soil cascading across the antique rug. A sob caught in her chest and she crouched down, furiously scrabbling the clumps of dirt back into the small pot.

"Kate." Brett crouched down beside her, then closed his big hands over her shoulders, urging her to her feet. "Leave it."

"I don't want to leave the mess," she whispered thickly. But his broad shoulder was so close and before she knew what she was doing, her face was pressed against it and his arms—oh, his strong, warm arms—had closed around her, pulling her against him.

Horrified, she scrambled backward, scattering the dirt even more. Vision glazed, she tried scooping it back into the pot.

"For God's sake, Kate. I said leave it. Mrs. Hightower will have it cleaned up. God knows she has plenty of staff under her thumb," he added flatly.

Kate dashed the dirt hurriedly into the pot, then brushed her fingers together. "You always detested

Mrs. Hightower,'' the words came without volition and her ears felt like they were on fire.

"She detested me,'' Brett countered smoothly. "Here. Stop blubbering.''

Shock propelled her to her feet. "I *don't* blubber.''

"Spoken with all the dignity of the princess of the manor.'' Brett's glance flickered over her as he returned the more-or-less restored pot to the shelf. "Except you've got mascara running down your face.''

Her stomach ached. "You're hateful.''

He shrugged, his disinterest plain. "Wipe your eyes, Katy.''

Katy. The name that only Brett had ever called her. She closed her eyes. For an aching moment, time seemed suspended. Bittersweet and filled with the ghosts of the past.

She turned away from the memories. And from his eyes that had always seen too much, yet not enough.

Then he pushed a soft, white handkerchief into her hand, and the aching moment passed. "Trust you to have a handkerchief,'' she murmured thickly. He'd always carried one. Even when they'd both been only thirteen years old, tearing up the schoolyard with their antics.

"My mama may have been a servant in a big old house not too far from here, but she did raise me with some manners.''

His oh-so-smooth voice grated. "And I'm sure all the women whose tears you've tenderly mopped throughout the years have greatly appreciated it.'' She scrubbed her cheeks. Hating him. Hating the situation that had brought him back into her life.

"Well, well, Kate. Jealous?''

She very nearly snorted. Only a lifetime of minding

her manners prevented it. "Hardly. I'm not the jealous type." That was a bald-faced lie and she was grateful that he didn't challenge it. She *had* been jealous. Jealous of the one great love in Brett's life. And she'd had no one to help her deal with it.

She'd needed a mother.

But Kate had been raised to believe that her mother had drowned in Stockwell Pond nearly thirty years ago. Caught between pond and lake, it was thirty feet deep in some places, two miles across at its widest point. Willows and oaks crowded along its jagged coves and inlets.

She wiped her eyes. She may hate the situation—hate *him* even—but there was a purpose to his presence. One she'd do well to remember. He was supposed to be a crackerjack investigator, after all. And that was his *only* purpose there.

"It can't be a painting of me," she said, forcing herself to think straight. "It's just…a coincidence. It has to be her…other child." A child who would have been only a year or so younger than Kate. A child who'd grown up *with* a mother.

Brett's silence spoke volumes and her fingers tightened around his handkerchief. "Why would my father lie all these years about my mother?" The question that had plagued them all for weeks, months, burst from her. "I never knew her because of him. I knew he was a cold, cruel man. But this—" She couldn't continue.

"That's why you and your brothers hired me," Brett reminded. "To help you find your mother. To get the answers that Caine can't, or won't give."

"*I* didn't want to hire you," she said, perturbed at the way he still managed to unsettle her.

His shoulders moved. Amused? Annoyed? She'd

given up trying to figure his thoughts long ago. "No kidding."

"But I'm told that you do own the best private investigative agency in the entire Dallas area."

"Not just in the suburb of Grandview?" Brett commented dryly. "I'm wounded."

"Jack suggested it some time ago. Then Caroline." Caroline Carlyle Stockwell. Rafe's brand-new wife. The mother of Rafe's brand new child.

"I get the hint. I'm here to find your mother. To do a job."

"Make sure you remember that."

His expression didn't change. "What's the matter, Kate? You afraid I can't keep my mind on the job what with being back amongst the exalted Stockwells?"

"Nobody knows better than I do that *nothing* distracts you from your work. I'm just curious why you accepted this case in the first place." Her lips felt dry. "Considering everything."

"You mean considering *you.*"

"That was a long time ago."

His gaze drifted over her. "You don't trust me," he said softly.

Her lips parted "I—"

"That's it, isn't it? You don't believe I'll do my best for your family."

"My brothers wouldn't have brought you in on this if they thought that."

"We're not talking about your brothers."

"No," she said after a long moment. "We're not."

"Well, well," he mused. "Score one for fierce Katy Stockwell." His eyes narrowed and his lips twisted a little. Just enough to make him look even more saturnine. "It'd have more effect if you weren't in tears, I'm afraid."

"Stick to the case, Brett. Find Madelyn LeClaire."

"And stay away from you."

"I didn't say that."

"You didn't have to."

She cursed the tears that still insisted on leaking from her eyes. "Jack didn't come all the way home from Europe with that…that painting, and call you here today just so I could cry on your shoulder." Her voice was flippant. Better that, than anything else. She couldn't bear it that this man, of all people, should see her weakness.

"I'll consider it my perk for the day." He didn't look any more delighted about it than she felt. "Look," he said after a moment. "You don't have to pretend that this hasn't been rough on you. First you learn that your father's cancer is terminal, then that your mother may be alive. And now, to see that portrait— Katy, it would shake anyone. You don't have to hide it. Hell, it shook me."

"Nothing shakes you."

His lips tightened. "You'd be surprised. Besides. I remember you at that age. You were a holy terror, and the girl in that painting looks as serene as a lovely country pond."

"Go away," she said flatly. "I need to fix my face."

"Is that a dismissal, princess?"

She shot him a look, prepared to give him a stinging reply, but the words died as she looked at him. "I don't imagine any one dismisses you," she said instead. Not anymore. He was too commanding. Too self-sufficient. And the cynical tilt of his lips was just a little bit fearsome.

The teenager who'd earned spending money working in the same house where his mother was the live-in cook for Judge Orwell and his perfectly coiffed wife, Bitsy, was long gone.

Now, Brett, in his beautifully cut summer-weight suit looked as if *he* might have a host of servants in his home at his beck and call. Which reminded her that, aside from knowing about Brett Larson, owner of a very well-respected private investigation and security firm, she knew very little about Brett Larson, the private man.

A fresh knot tied itself in her stomach. ''I—''

''Don't sweat it, Kate. We'll both forget this tête-à-tête ever happened. No one will ever learn from me that Kate Stockwell possesses tear ducts.''

Kate's tears ceased. ''Remind me *why* I ever wanted to shackle myself to you. Oh, wait. I remember. It was that scintillating sense of humor.'' She listened to the cutting tone of her voice with something akin to horror. That wasn't her talking. She wasn't a cold, cutting woman.

She was an art therapist, for pity's sake. She spent her life *helping* people. Troubled children, most specifically. She didn't engage in verbal warfare with others.

Brett leaned over and looked in her face.

It took everything she possessed not to back away. ''What are you looking at?''

He straightened and shrugged, disinterested. ''Just seeing if that bit of vulnerability ran off your face along with the mascara and makeup.'' Then he smiled humorlessly and walked out of the sunroom.

Kate's hands curled. She angled her chin and glanced around the sunroom. It was filled with carefully tended plants, antiques, comfortable furnishings. The Texas sun shafted diagonally in through the windows, golden and bright and warm.

One might actually think the house she stood in was filled with that same warmth. But she knew differently. Her cold and cutting father had seen to that.

"Damn you, Caine Stockwell," she murmured under her breath. He was her father. She knew that a part of her loved him, despite everything. But another part, a part she felt guilty in admitting to, detested him. For his coldness and abusiveness to his family. For his manipulations. For his lies.

The biggest lie of which had brought Brett Larson back into Kate's life.

Her hands were shaking again. She drew in a long breath and went into the hall, stopping to check her reflection in one of the framed mirrors that hung on the wall, along with an extensive collection of paintings. Stockwell ancestors. Oils. All originals. Her father would never have settled for anything less hanging on the hallowed walls of his mansion.

Her eyes looked a little red-rimmed, but she didn't have mascara running down her face.

Other than that, she looked much like she always did. Dark brown hair. Blue eyes. A face that was too narrow, a nose that was too long. Overall, she guessed she was presentable. There had even been a time when Brett had called her beautiful, and she'd believed it. Felt it.

But that time was past. Long past.

Now, she was just a woman who tried to help other people's children deal with their problems. She was successful enough at it, found it fulfilling and rewarding enough that, usually, she managed to forget what she really was.

A useless shell of a woman.

She looked down and realized she still held Brett's handkerchief crumpled in her fist. She pressed it to her cheek for a moment. Smelling the seductively male scent of him that clung to the folded, pressed-edged, square.

She was also a member of the Stockwell family, she reminded herself silently. She'd been part of the decision she and her brothers had made to right as many of the wrongs committed by their father as they could. And part of that meant finding their mother. *If* she really was still alive, as their findings suggested.

She sighed and turned toward the study once more. And nearly jumped out of her skin when Mrs. Hightower appeared silently behind her.

Kate cleared her throat and slid the handkerchief into the hidden pocket of her slacks. ''Did you need something, Mrs. Hightower?''

The woman's smooth expression didn't indicate in the least whether she recognized the vestiges of tears in Kate's eyes. ''Your office is calling,'' she said.

Kate's mind shifted to the calls she'd made earlier. She thanked the housekeeper and turned back to the sunroom and the phone extension there.

With any luck at all, the call would bring good news for her young patient, who was so close to a breakthrough if only his father would stand firm against his controlling family who seemed to want nothing more than to shut the boy in his bedroom and pretend he didn't exist.

She didn't want to fail little Bobby.

She knew it was unwise to become so emotionally vested in a patient, but there was something about the dark haired, sloe-eyed little boy that had stolen her heart.

Yes, as a woman, Kate was pretty well useless.

Which meant being a therapist was all she had left.

Chapter Two

Was there ever a woman put on this earth who drove him nuts the way Kate Stockwell did? If there was, Brett didn't want to meet her.

He ran his hand down his face and battled down the annoyance inside him before walking back into the Stockwells' study where Kate's brothers were still discussing the portrait. If they'd even noticed his and Kate's absence, they made no sign of it.

Then he realized that Jack was watching him. Kate's oldest brother had noticed all right. But then Jack had always seemed to have an extra dose of protective instincts where his sister was concerned.

And even though Brett had once been as comfortable around her brothers as he'd been around her—when he'd been just one more of the gang—he knew those times were gone.

He was the ex-fiancé of their baby sister and he had

no doubts that Kate hadn't left any question in her brothers' minds about who was at fault for the "ex" part of that particular equation.

He wasn't part of their group any longer, if there even was a group. Jack seemed to spend most of his time in Europe, as far as Brett knew. Rafe was a Deputy U.S. Marshal now, and Cord had taken over the family business interests. And Kate. Well, Kate had returned from Houston a few years ago, after her divorce from a man who'd once been Brett's friend.

Brett remembered the exact day he'd heard she was back in Grandview. That she'd moved back into Stockwell Mansion. He'd blown his cover on a case he'd been investigating and it had taken two solid weeks to regain the ground he'd lost that day.

No. Brett definitely wasn't here because of his former ties to this family. He was only the investigator they'd hired to follow the leads they'd already discovered regarding their mother. And since that's the way he liked it, he needed to stop thinking about his past and focus instead on Madelyn Johnson Stockwell's past.

"Were there other paintings of hers in the gallery where you found this one?" he asked Jack.

The other man shook his head. "Not anymore. I'd just missed a seascape that he'd had for a brief time. Beyond that, what there was had already been sold. Her work seems to be in fair demand over there." His lips twisted. "And has been for years. The only reason this portrait hadn't been sold to a private party was that the gallery owner, Roubilliard, didn't want to part with it."

"Then why did he?" Cord asked.

"Made him an offer he couldn't refuse."

"Bought him off, you mean," Rafe translated.

Jack shrugged. "It doesn't belong hanging on an art

gallery wall in France. It belongs hanging on the walls
of this house, along with the other portraits of the Stockwells."

"It would've been, too, if we hadn't been fed that
garbage about Mom drowning with Uncle Brandon,"
Rafe said grimly.

Brett watched Jack's face. He was the eldest and naturally would remember more of that day when Caine
Stockwell had planted the seeds of a lifelong deception.
But Jack's expression didn't change. He merely reached
for a pile of brochures and held them out to Brett.

"Here," he said. "Madelyn LeClaire's work is listed
in several of these catalogs. Private shows. Group
shows. A couple of estate auctions."

Brett took the items, fanning through them. Some
dated back fifteen years. He suddenly knew Kate had
entered the room behind them, but kept his attention
front and center, where it belonged. On the job.

That lasted about half a second. He looked back at
her. Frowned a little at the drawn expression on her
face. She looked even worse than she had when he'd
left her in the sunroom.

Dammit.

He didn't want to care how all this was affecting Katy
Stockwell. He deliberately looked down at the catalogs
in his hand and paged through them once more. The
job. Remember the job. "Quite a collection," he murmured.

"People tended to hang on to them. And I think the
owner of that—" Jack lifted his chin toward the portrait
sitting against the wing chair "—had a bit of a crush
on the artist. He's the one who said he was certain she
was living somewhere in New England and that she was

being represented by a dealer in Boston. But that information is a few years old, at best.''

"But it proves something, at least," Rafe said flatly. "Our mother *is* alive. She didn't die in a boating accident. Not here. Not anywhere. Just like we figured after what Caroline and I found in her father's papers. Did your smitten gallery owner happen to say what she looked like, since Caine saw fit to get rid of any photographs of her?"

"No. But we've all heard often enough from other people who knew our mother how much Kate resembled—*resembles*—her."

"Well," Brett said, "since you've brought me in on this, I've had my people checking the usual sources to locate a Madelyn LeClaire living anywhere in the New England area. No luck. If she *is* living there, she's doing it very quietly. Most people leave some footprints of their life. Driver's licenses, mortgages, property taxes, library cards. Something. But there's been zilch, so far." And in his experience, when people lived that quietly, it was for reasons they generally didn't want to advertise.

He looked at Jack. "Are you sure your Roubilliard in France was certain of his facts?"

"The guy had a major case for her. I'm sure," Jack answered.

"Then it's time for a road trip to Boston. Check the art dealers in person," Brett said. Although each of the brothers had done a lot of legwork, amassing enough information from the sketchy details they'd been given by their father in one of his rare lucid moments, he knew they had lives to lead. While his life was his work.

Which was why he'd been hired. The Stockwells had insisted that he personally take the case even though he had a half-dozen investigators on his staff who could've handled what was, essentially, a missing persons case. Even though it would have been easier, wiser, all the way around for someone else to deal with this family other than he.

"My office has already gathered information on the most likely galleries to be dealing with your mother. It'd be an easier task, except that she worked in so many mediums. Painting. Pottery. Sculpture."

He'd hoped, actually, to accomplish more without having to make the trip. God knew he had no desire to go to Boston ever again. But they'd met with one dead end after another. It was as if the artist named LeClaire was protected by some unspoken shroud of discretion. Dealers knew *of* her, but nobody would offer more information than that.

"You can handle the trip, right?"

Brett answered Rafe's question with a terse nod. "I had my secretary juggle my schedule for the next few weeks, just in case something like this came up. I can leave tomorrow morning."

The other men nodded, satisfied. Cord, after another look at his watch, excused himself to rejoin his wife.

"Surely it won't take that long? Weeks?" Kate moved nearer, bringing with her that faint feminine scent that was uniquely hers.

Brett shrugged, ignoring the surge in his bloodstream. "Probably not. But there are dozens of galleries and art dealers in Boston alone."

"And you don't just handle contacting them by phone?"

He looked at her, keeping his temper with an effort. "I've already said we've done as much by phone and the internet as we can. Now it's time to personally visit the galleries. Don't worry, Kate. All expenses will be accounted for in detail when the case is concluded.''

"I wasn't implying anything."

He raised one eyebrow. He knew better and it rubbed him wrong how little she trusted him. "Really?"

Her lovely blue eyes suddenly snapped at him. "It is *our* mother you're searching for." She waved her elegant, long-fingered hand to encompass her brothers. "Is there some reason why we shouldn't be interested in *how* you intend to find her?"

"Kate."

"No, Jack. I want to know." Her gaze stayed on Brett.

"While you two kids battle this out, I'm gonna go steal my wife away for a hot afternoon date," Rafe drawled, amused. He nodded sympathetically at Brett and gave his sister a wide berth as he left.

Jack, Brett noticed, just leaned lazily back against the bookcase, apparently prepared to enjoy the show.

"First of all, I'll continue weeding out galleries and dealers who clearly don't handle Madelyn LeClaire's type of art." He forced himself to remain patient. He'd never before been annoyed at explaining the manner in which his investigations were conducted. Which meant it was just *her* questions that annoyed him.

"Well, *I* could do that," she pointed out smoothly. "What else?"

"Then I'll take a photo of that portrait sitting there and these catalogs—" he held them up with exaggerated patience "—and personally canvass the remaining list."

"Okay, enough." Jack apparently recognized that Brett was speaking through his teeth by now.

"But—"

"Enough, kiddo. Brett's the best at what he does. And it's time to let him do it. Agreed?"

Her lips tightened. "Except for one thing." Her gaze returned to Brett. "I'm going with you to Boston."

"What?" Jack stared at Kate.

Brett shook his head. "No."

"I can help you," she said and he was painfully aware of the edge of desperation in her voice. "You said there were dozens of galleries," she reminded needlessly.

"I work alone." It was close enough to the truth. "If I didn't, I'd take someone from my office. Not you." He didn't want to go to Massachusetts at all, much less with *her* on his heels. Not even if he had to check out fifty galleries.

"I don't think it's up to you to make that decision."

"Listen up, princess." He saw her chin lift at the name. "You're not gonna tell me how to run my case. If that's the way you want to proceed, find another investigator, because I'm outta here. Understand?"

She moistened her lips. Turned to her brother. "Jack—"

"Brett's right." Jack pushed away from the wall. "His case. His job. His way."

"But—"

"You wouldn't want someone coming in to one of your sessions and telling you how to do your job, would you?"

Brett watched Kate's expression falter and couldn't help but wonder at the cause. A Kate who argued and laughed was a Kate he knew. A Kate who looked stricken and uncertain was another thing altogether. Nor did he need Jack to enforce Brett's rules, but he did find it enlightening to watch Kate.

Or maybe, despite everything, he just liked watching Kate.

She was stubborn and contrary and bossy as hell.

She was also a tall, blue-eyed beauty, and standing there—her slender body clad in that silvery blue suit that clung to the high curves of her breasts and the completely female curve of her hips—she was completely distracting. The vulnerability barely hidden by the passion vibrating from her was enough to make a man want to sit up and beg.

Another man. Not him. He'd already ridden that ride, thanks.

"No, I wouldn't want someone interfering with one of my therapy sessions," she admitted, her voice husky.

"Okay, then," Jack said, as if that settled the matter. Then his expression seemed to soften a little as he studied his sister. "You sure you want to do this?"

Kate nodded, and it seemed to satisfy Jack, because he turned to Brett. "Brett. Good luck. Keep in touch."

Brett nodded, still watching Kate, and the other man left the room, too.

Kate's blue gaze slid to Brett and he leisurely adjusted his focus from her hips. Her cheeks were flushed when he finally looked at her face.

But at least she'd nearly lost that *lost* look.

"Must be nice to be able to call the shots with your schedule," he said. "Most people don't have the luxury. Particularly psychologists."

"I'm an art therapist," she said flatly. "I work in partnership *with* psychologists and psychiatrists. And you control your schedule, too. So don't stand there and act as if it is something to be ashamed of."

"Feeling a little defensive, are you?"

To his secret relief, the last bit of *lost* disappeared from her eyes.

"Not in the least," she assured coolly. "But at the moment, I am between patients. And I *do* intend on going to Boston."

"Because you don't trust me to do my job."

"*Will* you?" Her voice was husky and it made his nerves tighten. "You hate me. I can see it in your face."

"You overestimate yourself, Kate. And as you've said, nothing gets in the way of my work."

She seemed to wince a little. "Then I'll go to Boston by myself."

"And do what?"

"I can talk to gallery owners just as easily as you can."

"You're right. Go hunting through the art world yourself. Spread that mighty Stockwell name of yours as far and wide as you like. And if your mother *doesn't* want to be found, which seems kinda likely if you ask me after nearly thirty years, once she hears a Stockwell is looking for her, she could well go to ground and you and your brothers would be lucky to pick up her trail ever again."

She blanched and swayed.

He swore and pushed her down on a chair, summarily pushing her head down. "I don't need you passing out."

She scrabbled at his hand. "Get your hands off me. I am *not* passing out."

He was perfectly happy to remove his hand from the slick silk of her hair.

She shot out of the chair, her hair tossing about. Almost as if she was afraid he'd have the gall to put his hands on her again. "I'm going to Boston," she insisted.

"Why?" Because she didn't trust him to do his job. The knowledge sat like a bitter pill. "Or maybe you really are enamored of my company once again," he needled.

Her eyes flashed. "Oh, please. Don't flatter yourself. If you must know, it's because...because my brothers have all done something to help find our mother, and I've done nothing!"

"Come again?"

She pushed her fingers through her hair and walked over to the portrait, her expression telling him that she already regretted her flash of honesty. But she surprised him when she didn't clam up the way he expected her to.

"Cord was the one to discover that Daddy was sending huge sums of money to one of his attorneys and had been every month since our mother supposedly died when I was a baby." She recited the details without emotion. "He's also the one who found a letter from my mother's side of the family, the Johnsons, in Daddy's personal records implying that the Stockwell side had once swindled the Johnsons out of land on which the Stockwells eventually discovered oil. And he's been looking into *that* so we can make it right again, if it is true."

She rubbed her fingertip along the frame of the portrait. "Rafe, now, he followed the money. To Clyde Carlyle's office. And between him and Clyde's daughter, Caroline, they found the divorce papers between my parents which were dated months *after* Madelyn supposedly died. They're the ones who learned that Madelyn, and Uncle Brandon, too, most likely, spent a considerable amount of time in France, moving here and there. And that, somewhere along the way, she'd apparently changed her last name to LeClaire.''

"And Jack, being the most familiar with Europe because of his travels, picked up the reins at that point," Brett concluded. He'd heard it all before from her brothers. But he'd never really thought how Kate may have felt about not having as active a role in the discoveries as her brothers.

Then he reminded himself that he was no longer interested in what went on inside her pretty head. Which mattered not at all considering the way her oddly false calm gnawed at him. "You think you'll be holding up your end by traipsing around Boston with me."

She nodded silently.

Brett swore inwardly. He still didn't know why he'd accepted this case in the first place. It was gonna be one huge headache. Not only did she not trust him, but she was trying to salve her conscience. "Kate. You and me…it's not a good idea."

Her lips pressed together for a moment. "Because we used to be engaged.''

Because you drive me nuts. "Because I'm used to working alone.''

"I wouldn't get in your way.''

No, you'd just be a constant distraction. Things might be dead and gone between them, but he was still a man. And she was a beautiful woman. A woman who didn't trust him, no matter what her other reasons were. "No.''

She made a soft sound, her gaze still on the portrait. And he made the fatal mistake of moving around from where he stood, so that he could see her face.

Confusion. Hurt. Longing.

All of that was written on her perfectly oval, perfectly

formed face. It was in her eyes and in the soft lip that she'd caught between pearly teeth.

In the days since he'd become embroiled with the Stockwells' case, Kate had consistently been cool and controlled whenever they'd encountered each other.

And now, in one day—hell, in one *hour*—he'd seen her blue eyes swimming in tears, her aching so clear on her face that it beat his better sense into dust.

Swearing a blue streak in his mind, Brett *knew* he was making a mistake. "All right," he said, sounding anything but gracious. "We leave in the morning. I'll have my secretary, Maria, call you with the time."

Now her blue eyes were glistening again. And she was looking at him as if he'd just saved a kitten from the jaws of a rattlesnake.

"Thank you," she whispered.

He slapped the catalogs he still held against his palm. "Be ready on time," he said abruptly. "And don't go packing a dozen suitcases, either, princess. We're going there to work, not so you can walk around looking like a fashion show in progress."

Her expression changed. Her lips parted, furious.

But he was already walking out of the room, satisfied. Her fury he could handle. Her tears, obviously, he couldn't.

Chapter Three

She was late.

Brett would be by soon and Kate had yet to finish packing.

Yet where was she? In her room packing?

No.

She was standing in the wide arch of her father's bedroom, struggling with the urge to turn around and leave. The room was dark, the heavy velvet drapes at the windows drawn against the morning sky.

She shouldn't have left this task so late, she thought. Visiting her father when she felt so uneasy about going to Boston with Brett was probably not the wisest course, but he *was* her father. She was a Stockwell. And Caine, for all of his many faults, had drilled into his children the fact that Stockwells looked after their own.

She moistened her lips and entered the room. She quietly greeted Gunderson, her father's primary nurse, and approached the hospital bed that was situated in the center of the cavernous room. Caine lay back against the white bedding. The muscular, wide-shouldered build that he'd passed on to his sons was wasting away on Caine; he looked much older than his sixty years.

She sat down on the chair beside his bed. His eyes were closed, but when she tentatively touched his hand, his head moved and he looked at her. "Hi, Daddy."

If Caine recognized her, he gave no indication. She'd visited him every day—except when he'd still been strong enough to tell her to go away. She'd told herself that his actions then had been because his pride didn't want her seeing him in his condition; but a part of her knew it was just as likely because he didn't want to be bothered with her.

"Gunderson?" She looked over her shoulder at the man. "I'd like to be alone with my father for a moment, if you don't mind."

He looked as if he did mind, but he nodded after a moment and left.

Kate turned back to face her father. "I'm going to Boston this morning," she told him. "With Brett Larson."

She saw Caine's lip curl, still managing to communicate his derogatory feelings without a word. He'd always treated Brett as if he weren't fit to step foot on Stockwell property. He'd been appalled when, at only twenty years of age, Kate had announced flatly to him that she was planning to marry Brett.

She swallowed and gathered her thoughts. This wasn't about Brett. It was about Caine's lies. About finding their mother. "We're going to find Madelyn," she continued, and at that, Caine's eyes flickered.

Though she'd promised herself that she was finished

with tears, they burned, threateningly near. She'd cried more in the past twenty-four hours than she had in years. And now she struggled with tears and the need to escape. She'd always felt a sense of fearsome awe for her father; now she felt pity and a hundred other emotions too tangled to define. "We've been a disappointment to each other, Daddy. You and I, both. But I—"

Beneath her hand, his fingers curled. "Madelyn? You came back to me."

She bit her lip, dropping her forehead onto their hands, praying for strength. It wasn't the first time Caine had mistaken her for her mother. She heard a rustle behind her and knew that Gunderson had decided that she'd used up her allotment of privacy. She lifted her head and looked again at her father. "I just wanted to tell you about my plans."

"Leave." The word was an order, despite the sigh that shuddered through his frail form.

She wondered if it was because, in his delusions he'd taken her for Madelyn, or if he knew it was his daughter he was ordering away. Sadly, it mattered little. She rose and began to walk from the room. Yet when she reached the archway, she paused. Looking back at him. There were so many things she wished had been different.

She drew in a shuddering breath and walked back to Caine's bedside. She gently smoothed his sheet over his chest. Then leaned over and pressed a soft kiss to his cheek.

"Goodbye, Daddy. I do love you."

She realized she was waiting for a response from him that would never come. Not even if he'd been physically able. Particularly if he'd been physically able.

Swallowing, Kate straightened and walked blindly

from the room, stopping short at the sight of Mrs. High-tower.

"You have another call," the other woman said, handing Kate a cordless phone, then turned on a silent heel and glided away.

Kate held the phone, feeling rather like a child who'd been caught receiving phone calls after curfew. She'd been fielding calls all morning, taking care of last minute details with her associates.

She sighed, glancing at her watch. Brett would be arriving any minute, and she still had to complete her packing.

She hurried to her bedroom, pushing the button on the phone as she went. "This is Kate Stockwell," she greeted, half afraid it would be Brett, calling to tell her he'd changed his mind after all. But hearing the voice of Bobby Morales's father, Kate knew that the garment bag, open and empty on her bed, would have to wait a little while longer.

She was late.

Brett looked at his watch again and climbed out of his car. He looked up at the set of windows on the second story that overlooked the front grounds.

Kate's windows.

At least they used to belong to her bedroom suite, he amended silently, remembering the day when he'd climbed up there and sneaked through her window just to leave her a rose on her pillow. For all he knew now, she could be occupying one of the pool cabanas out back.

But as he watched the windows, he saw a shadow pass by them and knew by the tightening at the base of his neck that it was Kate. Probably packing stuff she'd never need, he thought, as impatient with himself for agreeing to let her go to Boston as he was with her for being late.

He glared at the upper-story windows. Very nearly reached over the car door to lay on the horn. He had no particular desire to go up into the house to collect her.

House.

The place was called Stockwell Mansion. And a mansion it was. An enormous, cold mansion inhabited by a coldhearted man.

There were few people that Brett could say he truly hated. But Caine Stockwell headed the list. And because of it, Brett knew he probably shouldn't have accepted this particular case. He also knew that, because of it, he did accept this particular case.

He looked at his watch again then headed for the door. He didn't bother ringing the bell. He'd had to stomach enough glares from Emma Hightower across the threshold over the past few days to last him a lifetime. She'd made it abundantly clear that she figured he should still be using the servants' entrance in the rear.

Maybe it was high-handed, but Brett just pushed open the enormous door, and headed straight for the central staircase.

At the top, he turned unerringly toward the suite that Kate used to occupy. The door was opened and he could see her pacing back and forth across the thick carpet.

He also noticed the opened—but empty—suitcase sitting on the foot of her bed.

"Some things never change," he said, halting in the doorway.

She whirled, clearly startled as she pressed the phone clutched in her hands to her chest. "And some things do,'' she said, her tone frosty. ''I should have locked my door.''

''You oughta know that locks don't keep me out.''

''Breaking and entering. Sneaking up on people. Well, I suppose that's what a professional snoop does.''

''Don't turn up your pretty nose at that, princess,'' he said smoothly. ''My snooping is going to lead you to your mother.''

She frowned and turned away, tossing the phone onto the blinding white spread. ''Mrs. Hightower didn't tell me you were here already.''

''I didn't see Mrs. Hightower.'' He frowned at the way Kate was carefully arranging one thing at a time inside the suitcase from the neatly folded pile beside it on the bed. He walked over and joined her, reaching for the entire stack.

She gaped at him. ''What do you think you're doing?''

In answer, he plunked the clothing, stack intact, right into the case. ''It would take all day at the rate you were going. What else goes in here?'' He glanced around, expecting to see a stack of suitcases sitting somewhere already. The occasional trips they'd taken together years ago had always been accompanied by a minimum of three suitcases too many. All he saw, however, was one soft-sided tote sitting atop the white upholstered chair near the French doors. Shoes and makeup, he'd bet. ''Well? What else? This can't be all.''

''Why can't it?'' She countered.

He eyed her and she huffed, striding into the dressing room. She came out a bare minute later, diligently avoiding his gaze as she dropped a bundle into the case. All he caught was a glimpse of pastels and lace and silk before she quickly jerked the flap into place and yanked the zipper around, closing it.

"All right, I'm ready. Satisfied?"

"I would be if you weren't thirty minutes late." He grabbed up the bag and slung the strap over his shoulder.

She picked up a small purse that matched the coral-colored dress she wore and retrieved the smaller tote from the white chair. Then it was she who waited for him. "Well? I thought you were in a hurry."

"Where's the rest?"

"Rest of what?"

"Your suitcases."

She gave her tote bag an exaggerated jiggle, raising her eyebrows expressively. "Hello?"

"Come on, Kate. We don't have time for this."

"Then stop standing there, wasting more of it," she said, sugar sweet, and glided past him in a tantalizing swish of fragrance. "Like *I* said, Brett. Some things *have* changed."

He followed, thinking he'd be a helluva lot happier if he could count on that fact on every front, not just her apparent packing habits.

Outside the mansion, Kate stopped short at the sight of Brett's car parked in the driveway at the base of the wide entry steps.

Naturally, she thought. Gleaming black, long, low and wicked, the car was everything that he'd long ago vowed to own. He took the tote bag from her and she watched him dump the bags into the minuscule back seat. With his black-brown hair, shadowed jaw, and dark glasses that he slid into place before opening the passenger door, he looked wholly unfamiliar to her.

Dark. Dangerous. A perfect complement to the powerful car he drove.

Unsettled at the thought, she sank into the passenger seat and busied herself with retrieving her own sunglasses from her narrow purse. The top of the car was down, and the sun was killing despite the early hour.

"Fasten your seat belt."

Her lips tightened at the sharp pain that knifed through her. As if she needed a reminder? She shoved her sunglasses on her nose and snapped the safety belt into place. But still, Brett didn't start the engine. She looked straight ahead through the windshield. "What are you waiting for now?"

"You're awful edgy this morning."

She propped her elbow on the sun-warmed door beside her, unable to prevent a quick glance his way. "I don't know what you mean."

He still didn't reach for the ignition.

"Well," she said flippantly, "don't blame *me* if we miss the flight."

"We've got time," he said as he finally started the car and drove away from the house. "I told Maria to tack on an extra half hour since I know you've never been on time for anything in your life."

She sat back, stung. "I had a few calls. It couldn't be helped."

"Need to cancel your next manicure and pedicure?"

Her jaw ached. "As a matter of fact, yes. I also called my personal trainer and my masseuse. Made sure they knew I wouldn't be available for my daily sessions."

"Are you going to be this difficult from here on out?"

"Only if you're going to insult me every time you open your mouth." She exhaled wearily. What was it about this man that made her lose all semblance of civility? "I didn't mean to be late," she admitted reluctantly. "The father of a patient phoned."

"I thought you said you were between patients."

"I am." And she wasn't at all pleased about failing.

Fortunately Brett didn't pursue that point. She was still filled with frustration over the Morales case. She didn't need Brett digging at it, making it worse.

The wind rushed around them as Brett drove down the long driveway. The impeccably manicured grounds of the estate seemed to stretch out forever, as green as green could be. Grass groomed. Oaks and sweet gum trees towering. She rarely paid the grounds much heed, and probably wouldn't even today if it weren't a far safer subject to study than Brett and his low-slung, edgy car.

Not even Cord, who changed cars nearly as often as he changed his shirt, had a car like this one, she thought. And it was as different from her sedate, hard-topped sedan as it could be.

It also ate up the miles to the airport. It seemed barely minutes had passed when Brett pulled into a small lot where he parked under a numbered awning. He pushed a button and the car's top smoothly lifted into place.

"You always said you'd have a car like this one day," Kate murmured, smoothing her hand along the seat. "Is it new?"

"Had it a few years, now."

He came around and opened her door, then pulled out her luggage as well as his own bag.

She took her small tote from him and slid the strap over her shoulder as he locked the car. "How long is the flight to Boston?"

He shrugged. "A few hours or so."

Kate hurried to keep up with him as he strode out of the private lot, his long legs eating up the distance. At five foot eight, she wasn't short, but her stride was nothing compared to his. She finally quit trying, and walked at a more comfortable pace behind him as they entered the terminal.

He was arrogant and annoying and a workaholic.

And just because she'd cried her eyes out in front of him the day before as if she was eighteen instead of thirty, didn't mean her opinion on that had changed one bit. And just because she'd been unable to find sleep until the wee hours that morning, didn't mean that she'd been dwelling on it, either.

She quickened her pace again and nearly ran into Brett when he stopped to wait for her. He pointed her toward the check-in and stuck a piece of paper in her hand. "That's our confirmation number. I need to make a call. Can you handle checking us in?"

She wouldn't take offense. She wouldn't. So what if she had to count to ten? At least her voice was even when she answered. "I think I can manage."

He looked at her for a long moment. Then left her with the bags and walked away. She could see that he'd produced a slender cellular phone from somewhere.

Whether he wore a suit as he had yesterday, or looked rangy in blue jeans and a striped rugby shirt the way he did today, he was always at work. That was Brett.

Sighing faintly, she turned around again and waited for her turn. It didn't take long. She read off the number for the woman behind the desk, absently produced her driver's license for identification and glanced around the busy terminal. She hadn't flown anywhere in years. And she'd never been to Boston before.

"All right, ma'am. Your seat assignments have already been made—row thirty-two, with an aisle seat.'' She pushed Kate's bag and Brett's duffel onto the conveyor belt behind her.

"Row thirty-two?'' Kate focused. ''That doesn't sound like first class.''

The clerk blinked. ''No, ma'am. You're in coach.''

Kate shook her head, smiling. ''I'm sorry. That won't do.'' Brett would have to wedge his wide shoulders and long legs into a coach seat with a shoehorn. ''There must have been an error with the reservation or something. Is there any way we can upgrade to first class?''

''Well, yes, of course, ma'am. But the fare is considerably—''

Kate waved that away. ''Here.'' She opened her wallet again and pulled out her American Express. ''Will that do?''

The woman nodded. And in moments, she handed over a pair of new boarding passes. ''I'm afraid you don't have much time to get to the gate. Enjoy your flight.''

Kate smiled. ''Thanks.'' She tucked her credit card and the tickets into her purse and turned to find Brett already heading her way. He hustled them through the security check where it was obvious he was well-known, and onward to the gate just in time for the boarding call.

Kate handed over the boarding passes and they walked onto the plane. The smiling, blond flight attendant greeted them, and Kate stepped past her, heading toward their seats. She dumped her tote and purse on Brett's seat and slid into the one next to the window. Even in the spacious first-class cabin, she knew he'd want the aisle.

''Kate.''

She wriggled in the roomy seat and looked up at him. Then at her tote. She plucked her purse out of his seat and tucked it beside her. "My tote will fit in the compartment, won't it?"

He sighed. "What did you do?"

She looked at him. His expression was tight. All signs of humor gone. "You mean the seats? I switched them," she said easily. "You didn't really intend to sit back in the sardine section." A wave of uncertainty hit her. "Or…did you?"

He didn't answer her. He turned instead to the blond flight attendant who'd been looking at him like a cat eyeing a bowl of cream. "We need to switch seats out of first class," he told the woman.

He was serious. "Brett," Kate tried to get his attention, but he was seriously ignoring her.

"I'm sorry, sir," the blonde answered as if it was an everyday occurrence for someone to turn *down* first-class seating. "We're heavy today. All seats booked."

"We just gave up coach seats," he countered.

She shook her head. "Standby passengers have already been boarded. I assure you, sir, we are full. And you'll need to take your seat now."

Beneath their feet the plane gave a little lurch as if to agree with her words. "I'll stow that for you." She took Kate's tote and to her credit, her smile didn't dim a watt at Brett's grimace.

He sat down beside Kate and fastened his seat belt, then pulled some files from his briefcase before stowing it beneath the seat. Without a word to Kate, he flipped open one of the files and focused on whatever was inside it.

"Brett—"

His arm was resting on the armrest between them, and his fingers lifted. Warning.

She chewed the inside of her lip. Then finally turned and looked out the oval window as the plane backed away from the gate, then smoothly taxied around to join the line of planes awaiting takeoff.

She wondered for a moment if Brett remembered the time that she'd decided she'd wanted to be a pilot. She'd taken ground school classes before their senior year in high school and everything. Of course, that was back when she'd also thought it would be cool to be an actress, or a firefighter, and a dozen other careers that she'd fantasized about.

"Did you take your motion sickness stuff?" Brett suddenly asked.

Her eyes burned. "Before I left the house." It was already beginning to make her feel drowsy. And it was the motion sickness that she'd learned plagued her only while flying that had put a damper on her teenage enthusiasm for becoming a pilot.

"Good," he said flatly. "The last thing we need is you heaving your guts."

"Put ever so poetically," she murmured. She turned in her seat toward him. "Brett, I thought the seating thing was an error. We always traveled in first class."

"No, Kate." His voice was low, his tone flat. "You always did and just took me along for the ride. My clients don't pay for me to ride around in first class and limousines. They pay me for results."

Her lips firmed. "Well, I'm the client this time."

"I don't care if you're the Queen of England. I have policies and it doesn't include this. I warned you, princess, not to mess with my job, and already you're doing it."

Her lips parted, incredulous. "Because I didn't think you'd want to cram yourself into a seat with too little legroom for you to be comfortable?"

"Open your eyes, Kate. People do it all the time, every day. Including me."

"I was thinking of you," she countered over the sound of the engines revving.

"No, you weren't. You were taking over, adjusting the scenario until it suited your fancy, just like you always did."

"That's what you really think?" The plane was gathering speed as it headed down the runway.

His hard, square jaw tightened. "That's what I really think."

"Then it's a good thing we never made it down the aisle, isn't it?"

He looked back at his paperwork. "Seems to me you did make it down the aisle. With Hamilton Orwell the third."

Kate's stomach dropped as the plane suddenly lifted off the ground, heading sharply into the sky. But it seemed Brett wasn't through.

He looked at her, his expression unreadable. "Tell me, Kate. Were you sleeping with the guy who, next to you was supposed to be my best friend, at the same time you were sleeping with me? Or did he really sweep you off your feet into marriage in just those few months after you dumped me?"

Kate sat back like a shot, speechless.

"Nah," he mused. "Now that I think about it, I don't care."

She watched him turn his attention right back to the work spread out in front of him.

Of course he didn't care. He hadn't cared eight years ago. Not enough.

Her heart had been breaking because she'd finally acknowledged the truth about her standing in Brett's life. She'd been raised by a dyed-in-the-wool tycoon; a man who'd put his family last and his work first.

One of the hardest things she'd ever had to do was face the truth that she'd fallen in love with a man whose priorities were a mirror image to her father's.

For Brett, it was always work first.

Everything else, including her, had been last.

Chapter Four

Brett was glad that Kate nodded off halfway through the flight. At least while she was sleeping, he didn't have to see the wounded look in her eyes.

God. Why on earth had he agreed to take this case?

She'd asked the question, but he hadn't answered. Because he didn't have one. Any more than he had an answer to the insanity of letting Kate accompany him to Boston.

The flight attendant came by and refilled his coffee from a silver carafe. He looked at the china cup, sitting on the tray next to the case files he'd been reviewing.

Kate was like that cup. She was china. He was a foam cup.

She was champagne. He was a cold bottle of beer.

She came from a family whose name was synonymous with old Texas wealth and power. The man that left his mother alone and pregnant had been a drunk and a felon.

He looked over at her. Her coral-colored dress probably carried some fancy designer's name on it, even though it was nearly severe in its plainness. Just narrow straps over her lightly golden shoulders, a square top that hinted at the shadow between her breasts, and a brief length that displayed her long, sleek, bare legs. Even the simple ponytail she'd pulled her hair back into looked elegant and full of style.

She looked like the cover of some glossy magazine and he hadn't even bothered to shave that morning.

Well, he could drink his coffee from a china cup, and he'd learned to taste the difference between good champagne and bad. His firm even held season tickets for the ballet and the symphony. But he'd finally realized that no matter how much of the world he traveled over, how fat his bank account had become, or how much respect he'd earned, those basic differences in them would never change.

So it was probably just as well that Kate had chosen to marry good ol' Hamilton instead of Brett. If the two of them, both from the same social set, hadn't been able to make a marriage work, then it was a damn good bet that Brett and Kate together would've been one pure disaster.

The flight attendant came around again and collected his coffee cup, and Brett realized he'd been staring at Kate for so long that the plane had begun its descent.

He closed his briefcase and nudged Kate's arm with his. "Wake up, princess."

She murmured and shifted, curling up against his side, as if the armrests between them didn't exist.

He realized he was inhaling the scent of her like he'd

never breathed before. "Kate," he said sharply, annoyed with himself for getting into this situation, annoyed with her for smelling as sweet and fresh as a cool morning.

Her soft lashes lifted and she looked at him with a hazy expression. Her lips curved sleepily. "Brett."

That sleepy, sexy smile was like a jolt straight to his gut. The job, he reminded himself, coldly. Remember the job. "We're landing. In Boston."

Her eyes suddenly cleared and her cheeks went pink. She pressed her fingertips to her temple as she straightened in her seat.

He didn't know anyone anymore who blushed. Except Kate. "That stuff you take really knocks you out," he muttered.

"Mmm." She busied herself with her purse, not looking at him.

The plane touched down, engines screaming as it slowed. Brett released his seat belt and started to stand, but Kate touched his arm.

He waited.

"Brett, I think it would be…beneficial, if we agreed to keep our minds on finding Madelyn."

"You're telling *me* to keep my mind on the job?" His lips twisted at the irony. "Hold me down. I think the world might've just stopped spinning."

"I realize that might sound odd coming from me. But that's just my point. We still view each other as the people we were. If we could leave our—" she moistened her lips, hesitating "—our past *in* the past and concentrate on the present, on what we're trying to accomplish, our time here might go more smoothly."

"Act as if we're strangers. Who've just met."

"Well…yes."

The plane stopped moving and he got up and retrieved Kate's tote bag before the aisle filled with passengers. Then he looked down at her. "Can you do
that?"

She rose, smoothing her palms down the skirt of her
dress. Her eyes wouldn't meet his. "Yes, I can."

Liar. She could no more look at him and not be aware
of what had once been any more than he could. "All
right, then. Let's go. We've got a lot of ground to
cover."

She stepped out into the aisle in front of him and
walked off the plane. He followed behind, wondering
just how long she'd be able to make it last.

"We're not renting a car?" Kate stared at him as if
he'd lost his mind. "Why on earth not?"

They were outside the bustling airport, standing in
line, waiting for the next cab. He looked at his watch.
"Thirty-three minutes," he muttered.

"What?"

"Nothing. Look, Kate. Have you ever been to Boston?"

"No. But—"

"I have. Renting a car is a headache we don't need.
There's construction all over the place and parking is a
pain. We can walk to most places, and when we can't,
there's the T and cabs." A taxi pulled to a stop in front
of them and Brett pulled open the door for her. "Well?
Are you gonna trust me, or do you want to go back
inside the airport and catch a flight back to Dallas?"

She lifted her chin and for a long, drawn-out moment,
he thought she was going to argue. And if she did, he
would make sure she was on the first flight back to
Texas, and he would have some hope of peacefully go-

ing about his job. But her mouth stayed shut. She slipped past him and climbed into the cab.

He blew out a noisy, muttered oath, tossed the bags in on the seat and folded himself in beside her. He told the driver which hotel and sat back.

He hoped to hell they hit it lucky with the first few galleries. Otherwise, it was shaping up to be a hell of a long trip.

Kate pushed the bags around between her and Brett until they were right side up. One look at his profile was enough to tell her he was praying for the moment when he could pack her up and ship her away, out of his hair.

Well. She didn't want to give him any grief; she just wanted to help find her mother. She *needed* to help. She had to take some action, if only to help her live with the reality of her father's horrible lies.

She swallowed and gestured toward his briefcase. "Do you have a list of the art galleries we'll be visiting?"

"Yes."

"*Soooo*...do I ever get to see it?"

He flipped open his briefcase and pulled out a thick sheaf of papers and handed it to her.

Her jaw loosened as she paged through it. "This many? I thought you said you'd already eliminated some."

"I did."

"But there must be an art gallery on every corner!"

He laughed abruptly, but there was no real humor in it. "Yeah. A real cultural mecca."

Kate pressed her lips together. She focused fiercely on the list, reading each and every entry as if committing them to memory. It was better than dwelling on the shiver down her spine that his humorless laugh had produced. She managed to make the task last until the cab finally pulled to a stop in front of a multistoried hotel.

She looked around curiously as she climbed out of the cab after him. Though it was definitely warm, the air was still cooler than it had been at home and for the first time that day, Kate felt a little of her tension ease. Once she checked into her own hotel room and had a few minutes away from Brett, she'd surely get a handle on the taut, edginess that plagued her.

She sighed faintly, eyeing the expansive park across the street. Dozens of pedestrians walked by. It was busy and colorful and lovely, and under any other circumstances, she'd make plans first thing to explore the park.

"Planning to stand out here all day, princess?"

"Stop calling me that."

"Stop acting like one."

She wanted to slug him and the impulse shocked her. So, instead, she sailed past him through the hotel's beautiful entry, heading straight for the registration desk. She dropped her tote bag to the floor by her feet and smiled at the registration clerk. She'd barely opened her mouth to speak when Brett appeared at her side.

"Reservation for Larson," he said over her head to the clerk who nodded and began pecking at his computer.

"Yes, sir," the young man said after a moment. "I have that right here." He set a small form and a pen on the gleaming counter. "If you could just check the information and sign there, I'll make sure your room is ready for you."

Kate felt a jolt. "Ah...room?"

"Yes, ma'am."

Brett closed his fingers around her elbow, but she ignored the warning squeeze.

"*One*...room?"

"Yes, ma'am." The young man's eyes flickered uncertainly to Brett.

"Two rooms," she said firmly.

Brett's fingers tightened even more. "Excuse us for a sec," he told the clerk, and dragged Kate away from the desk.

She yanked her arm out of his grip. "I am *not* sharing a room with you," she said flatly. "I don't know *what* you think I was suggesting when I told you I was coming to Bos—"

"I'm not gonna jump your bones the second we're alone in a hotel room, so get over it."

Her cheeks felt on fire. "I am *not* sharing a room with you."

"Then you can take your pretty behind back to Grandview. It's August, Kate. Look around you. This place is crawling with people. You think I like the idea of sharing a room with you? Trust me. It wasn't my first choice."

"Then...get...a...suite."

"How can you be a therapist when you don't listen to a *word* anyone says? This place is booked as damn solid as the plane was."

She spun on her heel and strode back to the desk. "Could we get a two-bedroom suite, instead?" She reached for her purse and her credit card.

"I'm sorry, Mrs. Larson. We don't have anything available this week at all. There's a conference here, you see. Podiatrists." He shrugged apologetically, but Kate had stopped listening after being called *Mrs. Larson*.

Her brain simply shut off.

"If I see you pull out that bloody credit card, I'm gonna cut it in half," Brett murmured above her ear as he signed the registration form and pushed it back toward the clerk.

He palmed the narrow key card folder the clerk handed him and tugged Kate through the lobby toward the bank of elevators. Painfully aware of the looks they were receiving from the bellman who was carrying their few pieces of luggage, Kate waited until they were alone in their room.

Their room.

"Mrs. Larson?" She hissed the second the bellman pocketed his tip and shut the door behind him. "You registered us as Mr. and Mrs. Larson?" Her voice rose.

She watched Brett set his briefcase on the desk with extraordinary care. "Calm down."

"No! I won't calm down." How could she when the very notion of sharing a room with him was sending her nerves into shock. "What on earth possessed you? One room?" She turned and waved her arm at the room. "There's only one bed!"

"Quit acting like an outraged virgin," he said wearily. "It's a king-size bed. I can sure as hell control myself. Can't you?"

She pressed her hand to her forehead. "This is a nightmare."

"Then go home," he said flatly. "Because I guarantee you, Kate, I don't need *this*."

And he didn't need her. He never had.

"I just— I don't want to share a room. That's all. I'm used to my privacy."

"Yeah. That's why you live in Stockwell Mansion with your brothers and their new wives and families."

"Sarcasm doesn't suit you."

"And acting outraged and high and mighty is pretty damn tiring, too." He turned away from her, striding toward the wide bay windows at the end of the spacious room. He shoved his hands through his hair, looking very much like he wanted to tear it out by the roots. "Less than twelve hours," he muttered. "This case is gonna kill me."

"I'll find another room. If not in this hotel, then another. We drove by a half dozen on this street alone."

"No." He pushed open the glass doors and stepped out onto the small balcony that afforded the same view of the park as the hotel's entry.

She followed him. "I'm a grown woman, Brett Larson. What I decide to do and where I decide to stay is up to me."

"Not if it interferes with my case. And if you're so grown, start acting like it. We're here to work. I registered us as a couple for a reason, and if you'd stop overreacting for a second, I'd tell you about it."

The more reasonable he became, the more agitated she felt. "Shall I remind you that the only reason you *have* a case is because you're working for my family?" It was unconscionable. She knew it the moment the words left her lips.

His hard gaze settled on her face. There was no anger in his eyes. They were as deeply, darkly brown as they ever were—so dark she could barely discern the pupils. "That's it," he said evenly and turned back into the room.

"Brett. No. Wait. I'm sor—"

He'd picked up his briefcase and his suitcase and walked out of the hotel room, closing the door quietly behind him.

She stared in disbelief, then ran to the door and yanked it open, darting out into the wide, plushly carpeted hallway after him. All she saw, however, was the elevator doors sliding closed.

Dismay engulfed her. What had she done? Messed things up, but good, that's what. She went back into the room and snatched up her purse and the folder with the room key in it, then ran back out to the elevator.

She caught up with him only because he was waiting for a cab. Probably to take him back to the airport where he'd fly home to Texas and tell her brothers just what they could do with their case.

"Brett." She caught his arm. "I'm sorry."

He just watched her, his expression impassive.

"I am." She felt the muscles in his arm flex and she yanked back her hand, twisting it with her other around the strap of her purse. "Please, don't go. I shouldn't have said what I did. I acted…badly. Whatever rules you set, I'll follow."

His lips twisted. "That dog won't run, Katy. I know you too well." He stepped forward, reaching for the door of the cab that had just pulled to a halt at the curb.

"My brothers will never forgive me if I blow this!"

"Yeah, they will," he countered blandly. "They've always spoiled you rotten."

"I'm not spoiled."

His eyebrow rose.

"Okay, so they did. A little," she said hurriedly. "But you can't just leave me here, like this."

"Why not? Like you said, you're a grown woman. You're free to come and go wherever, whenever you please. Find your mother yourself." Then he climbed in the cab and a second later, drove away.

She stood there, staring stupidly after him.

''Mrs. Larson?''

She frowned, turning toward the doorman. ''What?''

''Are you all right, ma'am?''

''I…yes.'' She managed a smile. *Just fine and dandy, except I'm not really Mrs. Larson, and I've managed to alienate the one man my brothers had complete faith in.*

She couldn't continue standing on the curb without attracting even more attention from the doorman, so she went back inside the hotel. But heading to the elevator and going up to that empty room with the king-size bed was more than she could bear and she sank instead into one of the oversize chairs scattered around the gleaming lobby.

What was it about Brett Larson that reduced her from a competent, fairly even-tempered woman, into an absolute raving lunatic?

She rested her forehead on her fingertips. She'd have to call and warn her brothers what had happened. Brett would certainly let them know that he'd backed out of the case once he made it back to Grandview.

If there was a flight back to Texas soon, that meant she had only a few hours before the news hit and the shock waves spread this far east. Unless Brett used that handy, dandy cell phone he carried and lessened the time even more.

Her stomach churned just thinking about it.

She'd desperately wanted—needed—to do something *active*. Something productive in helping to find her mother, even if it meant having to deal with Brett.

So what was she doing sitting there, totally inactive, feeling sorry for herself?

There was nothing preventing her from going to the

airport after Brett. If she was careful, if she kept her big mouth shut, she could salvage this.

She straightened and strode out to the curb just as a cab pulled up. Perfect. A good sign.

The back door opened and a man climbed out.

A tall man. Broad-shouldered. With hair as dark as teakwood and eyes as dark as chocolate.

Her mouth parted. She was so glad to see him, she nearly threw herself into his arms. She actually took several steps toward him, curtailing the impulse just in time. She stared at him, a tangle of emotions nearly choking her. "I'm glad you came back."

He looked none too happy about it. He handed over his luggage to the doorman with a quiet word, then took Kate's arm in his. "We're going to get some things straight." He drew her, unresistingly, across the street toward the park. They walked a long while, as if he didn't trust himself to speak just yet. And she, she didn't know *what* to say. Eventually he found an empty bench and nudged her toward it.

"I've never walked away from a case yet, Kate." His shadowed jaw was tight. "And I'm not gonna walk on this one. But I swear, if we have to go through this kind of crap every day, I'll stuff a gag in your mouth and cuff you to the bedrail. Understand?"

She flushed. He was still so coldly angry that she could well imagine him carrying out the threat. "I'm sorry. I've said I'm sorry! You just…I, we…"

"Make each other crazy," he muttered.

She chewed the inside of her lip. "I didn't expect to have to share a room with you, Brett. It…threw me. I'm not proud of it."

Brett frowned. Kate had always been generous with her temper in the past, and equally generous with her apologies. "I think you were right," he said. "That we need to forget what we know about each other and concentrate on the task at hand."

"Well, obviously I was *so* successful at that. Thirty-five minutes, I believe you said."

"Thirty-three," he corrected.

"An even more impressive failure." She smoothed her hand over the stone bench beside her. "Brett? Do you really think she doesn't want to be found?"

The hard knot of anger inside him eased some at her diffident question. "Only Madelyn knows that, Katy."

He heard her sigh, then she stood, managing to look impossibly young and fragile for someone he knew had already hit the thirty-mark. He shifted his gaze, watching a pair of joggers passing by instead.

"Is it necessary to hide my name?"

"I've seen some weird things in my business. Someone overhears someone talking and the next thing you know, half the city is privy to a secret that only two people were supposed to know. From what I've learned, the art world is a small one. Word travels. I don't want to take any unnecessary risks."

"So you decided I should go by *your* name instead of my own."

"You're the one who insisted on coming here. If it weren't for that, we wouldn't need a cover in the first place. But since we do, it'll be a simple one. Newlyweds, looking for a new LeClaire piece to add to our collection."

"Newlyweds," she repeated faintly. "How... ironic."

"It's simple," he said again. He didn't want to think about ironies. He didn't want to think anything about the fact that they should have been newlyweds—for real—many, many years ago.

She worried her lip between her teeth for a moment. Then swallowed and spoke. "Why *did* you agree to take on this case, Brett?"

"It intrigued me," he allowed after a moment. "The Stockwells are an old, established family in Grandview. Obviously I like a mystery as well as the next guy, or I wouldn't be in the business that I am." She'd used to tease him about that. Called him a professional snoop.

"That's the only reason?"

He dragged his gaze away from her lips. "That's it."

"Mmm." She turned to go and he wondered if she saw through his lies as easily as he saw through hers.

"Kate."

She stilled and he walked around, in front of her. Where he could see her wary expression. "There is another reason," he told her abruptly. "I wanted to see if there was still anything to this." He ducked his head and covered her mouth with his.

Her jolt of shock passed through him.

Then, after an eternity of frozen heat, her fingertips whispered, light as air, down his unshaven jaw. She murmured his name.

Want, deep and dark and unending, rose inside him. He'd been stupid not to expect it.

Stupid to walk right into the flames.

He sucked in a harsh breath, flavored of her, fighting the urge to deepen the kiss. To take her mouth in the way that had haunted his dreams for too damned long.

He deliberately stepped back. Away. It took everything he owned to keep his hands at his side. To not reach for her again. To act as if his hair hadn't just been damn near singed off his body from the heat she roused in him.

She lurched a little. Her hand slowly lowered to her side. Her lips pressed together, as if she was savoring the sensation of their kiss. "Well," she said after a moment. Her voice sounded strangled. She cleared her throat. "Well."

Brett reached down and picked up the purse she'd dropped at their feet and handed it to her. "Now that we've got that out of the way," he said blandly, "do you think we can get some work done?"

Chapter Five

Kate closed her hands over the purse, clutching it to her with all her might. "Don't do that again."

His eyebrow peaked, making him look distinctly devilish. "Or what? You'll hit me with your purse? Tell your big brothers on me?"

"I think I could really hate you," she said, her voice low and shaking. The fact that he was clearly unmoved by a kiss that had made the foundation of her world tremble hurt more than she wanted to admit.

His lips twisted. "I thought you already did, Katy." He turned away, as if disinterested in continuing this particular thread.

Kate could either stand there, refusing to trot along behind him, or she could go with him. She could keep her mouth shut, pretend that he affected her as little as she affected him, and possibly—just possibly—get through the task set before them without completely losing her mind.

She slid her purse strap over her shoulder and followed him back through the park, across the street. He strode past the hotel entrance, however, and entered a crowded little restaurant a little ways down the street.

Lunch was a miserably quiet affair, despite the deli that teemed with diners. Brett didn't speak to her except to ask her to pass the mustard and to glare so fiercely at the sandwich she'd barely touched that she forced herself to swallow a few more bites of it. And when it came time to pay the bill, he glared at her as if she'd committed an unpardonable sin when she picked up her purse from the floor by her feet.

"I was just picking it up." She leaned across the table toward him and smiled coldly. "My wallet is still inside."

"Make sure it stays there," he said flatly as he dropped a few bills on the table and pushed back his chair to stand.

Kate tucked her tongue between her teeth, reminding herself that she was a reasonably calm, patient woman. She tucked her purse under her arm and decided to take her foam cup of lemonade with her since she hadn't yet finished it. She followed Brett back out onto the sidewalk, hurrying to catch up with his long legs.

"For a devoted new husband," she said, hating the way the sarcastic words emerged, "you're awfully anxious to ditch your bride."

He stopped cold and she nearly bumped into him. "You're right, *honey*." He put his arm around her shoulder and pulled her close to his side where she fit much too neatly beneath his arm. "Is this better?"

The smile that stretched his lips didn't reach his eyes

at all. But she would *not* give him the satisfaction of squirming out of his grasp. It was so easy to see that was what he expected her to do.

So she smiled back at him, mimicking his negative level of sincerity. She steeled herself to put her own hand around the back of him. To rest her palm against the hard, warm stretch of his long back. "So much better. *Honey.*"

And that is how they walked back into the hotel. The doorman from earlier smiled at them benevolently. The room clerk that had checked them in smiled at them, too.

"Everybody loves a pair of lovers," she muttered under her breath as they entered the empty elevator. She went to one corner and he to the other.

"If they only knew," Brett added expressionlessly as the doors soundlessly closed. He jabbed the button for their floor.

Kate twisted the strap of her purse and stared at the display over the doors. She felt about as jumpy as a cricket on steroids. She knew it was only because they were headed back up to that hotel room with the big, wide bed. "Remember when we got stuck in the elevator that one time?"

He looked over his shoulder at her. "I'm surprised you'd bring that up now."

"Why? There were so many of us...oh." Her face suddenly flamed. He was right. And her nerves had inadvertently opened up another can of worms.

"It was the night of the high school prom," he said flatly.

"You're right. I shouldn't have brought it up."

He turned and looked up at the floor display. Clearly he agreed.

The elevator ride should have been swift, but now, it seemed to crawl. Their prom night was twelve years in the past. It seemed ridiculous that she could recall every detail now so terribly clearly, when it had been years since she'd allowed herself to even remember that time in anything other than the haziest of ways.

She looked at Brett's back. He'd worn a pale gray tuxedo to their prom. She'd picked it out herself because she'd considered it a perfect foil for her pink silk gown. "You hated that gray tux, didn't you?"

"Yeah."

She sighed. She remembered that he'd owned one good black suit and that's what he'd wanted to wear. But when she'd insisted, he'd gone with her choice. "I'm sorry."

"It was a long time ago, Kate." He dismissed the apology, clearly bored with the subject.

And she was doing a miserable job of keeping the past in the past, she told herself when the elevator doors slid open and he stepped out into the corridor on their floor.

She followed him along the hall toward the room and wondered why—if it was so long ago—she could remember it so vividly.

Their clothing. The way he'd smelled of Old Spice. The nerves that had jangled in her stomach because she'd known that he'd reserved a hotel room and that they planned to leave the prom early and have their own much more private celebration.

Nothing had turned out the way she'd expected. Not their prom night, when they hadn't used the room because they'd gotten into an argument; nor the future they'd planned with such youthful arrogance.

He unlocked the door and pushed it open, waiting for

her to go in. Kate couldn't look at him. She walked past him, nearly wincing at the sight of that wide bed.

She heard the door close behind him and then he was moving past her for the table near the glass door. He dumped his briefcase on it and sat down, long legs sprawling as he flipped open the latches and pulled out a slender laptop computer. She watched him mess with various cords for a moment, then realized how foolish she must look still standing like a cardboard cutout by the door.

She picked up her suitcase that was sitting on the floor and set it on the dresser. The zipper sounded loud in the silence of the room and she could feel Brett's attention transfer to her for a moment. But when she couldn't stand it one moment longer and looked over at him, he was completely focused on his computer.

Her throat felt tight and she turned back to her un-packing. She drew out the task as long as humanly possible. But all too soon, she was done. She stored the suitcase on a shelf in the closet and looked around.

She could turn on the television, but she'd never been one much for watching TV.

She could turn on the radio, but with her luck, she'd probably get some station that played songs from a decade ago, and she'd be beset with memories of their prom again.

She very much wanted to ask Brett when he planned to start their rounds of the art galleries, but she couldn't bring herself to do so.

Instead she phoned her office to check her voice mail. But she'd apparently done such a good job with her calls earlier that morning that nobody felt a need to get in touch with her, for there were no messages at all. She called the mansion and caught Hannah for a few moments. Then, with no more calls to make, and still without enough nerve to prod Brett, she pulled out the paperback that she'd brought with her and settled gingerly on the edge of that wide, wide bed. She determinedly opened up the book. It was a romance. She loved reading romances.

Unfortunately the words didn't grab her. Not because of any lack by the author, who'd never failed on that score in the past, but because she was sitting on the edge of a bed that, come that very night, she would be sharing with a man who wished she was anywhere but here.

She couldn't take it one more moment.

She set aside the book and rose. "When are we going to get started?"

"Later."

She chewed her lip. "Why not now?"

He didn't look her way. "Because I'm busy."

"With what? Ignoring me in order to teach me a lesson?"

His jaw flexed. He continued pecking at the computer keyboard. It looked small compared to his large, square hands. Almost like a toy.

"Brett—"

He exhaled roughly. "Chill."

"I *beg* your pardon?"

"We'll start when I finish this."

"And what is *this?*"

"None of your business."

Her lips tightened. "Did we not already establish that you're working for my family?"

"Did we not already establish that you're here on sufferance?" He leaned back in his chair and looked at her through narrowed eyes. "Your case is not the only one I'm dealing with right now. Despite your belief otherwise, the world does not revolve around the Stockwell family.''

She supposed she deserved that. ''I thought you cleared your schedule for the next few weeks.''

''I did. But there are still some details that I have to deal with. And the sooner you leave me alone, the sooner I'll get them done.''

''What kind of case is it?''

''Missing person.''

''Like Madelyn.''

''Like a two-year-old child who was stolen from her custodial parent by a crumb of a father who has left the country and won't return until his wealthy wife coughs up a boatload of money in exchange for the kid,'' he corrected flatly.

Horror swept through her. She sank down on the edge of the bed, staring at him. ''Do you have many cases like that?''

He looked back at his computer. ''Too damned many,'' he muttered.

''This child…do you know where he is?''

''She. Yeah. I know. Getting to her is another matter.''

''Can't the authorities intercede or something? Surely—''

''Questioning the way I do my job?''

''No!''

''Sounds like it.''

''Maybe you're too sensitive.''

He laughed abruptly ''Oh, yeah. That's it. Sensitive.'' He shook his head. ''In this particular case, the area authorities are none too honest themselves.''

''So what are you going to do?''

He lifted his hands back to his computer. "We're gonna get the kid back to her mother. I've got a team on their way there. Barring disasters, that little girl will be in her mama's arms within a few days."

She looked at him, realization coming over her in a hard wave. "You would have been going with them if not for my family's search for Madelyn and this trip."

He didn't answer.

"Brett?"

He didn't so much as sigh. But she knew he wanted to. "What?"

"What's the child's name?"

"Does it matter?"

She blinked at the edge of fury in his voice. "I...well—"

His brown gaze lifted from his computer to focus on her. "Her name is Amy."

Kate absorbed that and felt an ache deep down inside her soul.

Amy and Adam. The two names that, a lifetime ago, she and Brett had chosen for the children they would one day have together.

She couldn't look at him. "I'm sorry for interrupting you," she managed to say. She picked up her purse. Slid her feet back into her shoes.

"Where are you going?"

"For a walk."

"Don't get any bright ideas of hitting up an art gallery or two."

"It didn't even occur to me."

"Right."

"It didn't." Her stomach felt tight. She needed fresh air. She needed a break from Brett. From the memories. From the reality of sharing this room with him. "If you must know, I thought I'd...take a walk and say a prayer for a little girl named Amy.''

Then, before he could say anything about *that,* Kate hurried out the door.

Brett watched the door close firmly after Kate's departing statement. Her voice had been thick with tears.

Going after her would solve nothing, he knew.

He let out a short, pungent oath, and wondered for the millionth time what insanity had brought him to this point.

She returned just before dark.

Brett tossed down the television remote and stood as soon as he heard the soft rustle and click outside the door. It opened and Kate walked in. Her hair was a little windblown. Her cheeks and the tip of her nose were a little sunburned. All in all, she looked vibrant and beautiful and perfectly safe.

It infuriated him. ''Where the hell have you been?''

Her eyes snapped wide. ''I went for a walk.''

''To where? Cape Cod?''

''I was giving you some privacy.''

''You've been gone for hours.''

''I don't need a keeper.''

''Could have fooled me.''

''I just walked around, Brett. I didn't slip inside one single art gallery.''

''No, you left here, obviously upset, and didn't return for hours.''

She carefully set her purse on the desk. ''I'm sorry. The last thing I intended to do was add to your concerns.''

She was completely sincere. He could see that in her face. He pulled in a calming breath and waited until he could speak without swearing at her. "Where did you go?"

"Well, if you must know, I visited a hospital. The pediatric ward."

He eyed her like she'd grown a second head. "What for?"

She shook her head, biting her lip. "I needed to be around children for a little while. That's all." She moistened her lips and smiled quickly. "It was funny, actually. I ran into a doctor I worked with a while back in Houston. We had coffee."

Brett could just picture it. Some rich doctor and beautiful Kate Stockwell. The feeling inside him came perilously close to jealousy and he ruthlessly clamped down on it. He never should have told her about the case with little Amy. And if he'd been able to get a lick of work done the day before after that damned meeting at the Stockwell mansion, he wouldn't have been working on it that afternoon.

"I ordered in dinner about a half hour ago," he told her evenly. "Steak. So if you want something lighter, you'll have to call it in yourself."

She made no move toward the phone. Perhaps she'd had food with her coffee and her old friend the doctor.

"Will you be notified when Amy is returned to her mother?"

He nodded and turned to the television. Kate said that name—Amy—and he felt something inside him tighten into a knot. He turned up the volume on the TV and sat on the foot of the bed waiting for the sports segment, wishing the sound could drown out the memories clanging noisily inside him.

After a moment, Kate scooted past him and sat down at the table with a paperback novel in her hand. He got a look at the cover as she passed by. Another one of those goopy love stories she'd always been fond of reading. Another thing about her that hadn't changed in eight years.

He listened to the weather report. Sunshine and more sunshine. Then sports. Nothing new there, either. Then the meal arrived. The steak that had appealed to him on paper was less appealing in reality.

Kate picked at her meal even more than he did. "I suppose it's too late to start on the galleries," she finally said.

"I suppose," he said pointedly, but felt no pride when her cheeks flushed.

"I'm sorry. I didn't mean to waste any of your time."

She hadn't. Not really. He'd made a lot of calls, checked in with some people he'd once known here in Boston and managed to eliminate a dozen galleries from the list without stepping foot from the hotel. It was his own bad luck that he'd been completely preoccupied with Kate's whereabouts. "Forget it," he muttered.

She looked as if she wanted to say more.

He was glad she didn't.

Eventually he gave up the pretense of eating and took refuge on his computer again, then his phone as he checked in with his secretary. That led to a host of other calls that kept his mind occupied. But when he saw Kate pull a familiar looking leather pad out of her bag, Brett felt every muscle in his body tense.

Her sketch pad.

She didn't look his way as she sat back down and flipped open the pages, holding it on her lap. She had an odd collection of pencils, all looking like they were of a different thickness, wrapped in a fat rubber band.

Brett could feel his nerves knotting as she selected

one of the pencils and set aside the others, then held the squat thing between her fingertips. His eyes focused on her wrist and hand. Looking so womanly, so delicate. He remembered seeing that delicate, feminine wrist wrapped in a metal contraption that looked like a torture device.

Remembered knowing that, because of him, her career as an artist was probably never going to happen. He hung up the phone, realizing that he'd been listening to a busy signal for too damn long. "You still sketch." The words came out of him. Unwelcome, unasked for, unsought.

Kate didn't look at him. "I always have."

Not always, Brett knew. Not when she'd been lying in a hospital bed, refusing to see him, with her delicate hand and wrist held together by pins and God knows what else thanks to the accident that *he* should have been able to prevent.

And if they were going to leave the past in the past, *that* was a seriously dangerous place to be loitering.

He swallowed an oath, wishing again that he were anywhere but here. Kate continued sitting with her sketch pad, hand eventually moving with the pencil over the paper.

He started to ask her if she still painted, but decided he didn't want to hear the answer. He wasn't going to open that door that had been closed for too damn long.

He couldn't see what she was sketching. She'd always been rabid about the privacy of her sketch pad. She'd told him that some people wrote in diaries. Some journaled. Some meditated and some prayed.

Kate sketched.

As he watched, the movements of her pencil seemed

to grow more steady, more rapid until it looked as if her hand was fairly flying across the paper.

He deliberately turned back to his computer. He was *not* going to get turned on by watching Kate sketch. By that intense absorption that overcame her while she was drawing, that intensity that was so similar to passion.

She sat at it for a long while, and he was numbingly grateful when she finally seemed to tire of it. She picked up the phone and dialed. Then he heard her low voice. She was talking to one of her brothers. The call didn't last long, and soon she hung up and gathered some stuff that she took with her into the bathroom. He heard the water running in the tub.

And knew his torture was only beginning.

He sat there, concentrating on work when the only thing his damnable body could concentrate on was the idea of Kate. Bubbles up to her chin. Sticking one long, shapely leg out as she lazily rubbed soapy lather from ankle on upward.

He shoved open the glass door and pushed one of the too narrow chairs from the table out onto the minuscule balcony. Then he sat down out there, propping his feet on the half-wall across from him and tilting his head back against the brick wall behind him.

He wished he had a cigarette, even though he didn't smoke any longer.

He wished he had a beer, though he never drank while he was on the job.

Most of all, he wished he was on the other side of the world, rather than the other side of a wall from impossible, willful and intoxicating Kate Stockwell.

Hiding out in the bathroom was about the most juvenile thing Kate could ever have imagined. She stayed in the bathtub for so long that the water went cold, and the bubbles were nothing but a memory. Her fingers and toes were like prunes.

She leaned forward and opened the drain, then wrapped a thick, fuzzy towel around herself as she stepped out of the water. She cleaned her teeth and her face. Rubbed lotion into her skin. Pulled on her pajamas. Restored order to the bathroom so that the only sign of her having been in there at all was the glisten of water clinging to the bottom of the tub.

None of it helped her forget the increasingly late hour, or the bed awaiting her.

None of it helped her forget anything.

Finally there was nothing else for her to do but leave sanctuary behind. She pulled open the door, absurdly grateful to see that the room was dark. A grainy black-and-white movie was playing on the television, the sound turned low. She could hear a car passing and realized the glass door was open. As her eyes adjusted to the darkness, she could also see Brett's long form propped awkwardly on a chair on the small balcony.

She started to turn away, but something about his form stilled her. He looked so alone.

Was he thinking about little Amy? The missing Amy, that was.

Probably. Brett had always been thinking about work. About making his mark on the world. About success.

You love your work more than you love me. The old refrain hovered in her mind. His work that would now, hopefully, lead to the return of a little girl to her mother.

Because of his work, his firm, a daughter would grow up with her mother.

Her throat felt unaccountably tight and she turned to

the bed, pulled back a corner of the bedding and gingerly tucked a pillow under her head.

She had spoken with the hotel manager when she'd arrived back at the hotel, and convinced him that it would benefit him greatly if they found a two-bedroom suite at the earliest possible moment for her and Brett to move into. With any luck at all, she and Brett would be stuck in this one-bed torture chamber for only a short time.

She bunched her pillow again. With any luck at all.

When she didn't hear Brett make a move from his position out on the balcony, she finally began to relax.

Her eyes sought out the red glow of the clock display. It was nearly midnight. The next day, their search for Madelyn LeClaire—or at least Kate's participation in the search—would begin for real.

The reality of it curled through her stomach. Nerves. She turned her cheek into the pillow.

Brett seemed perfectly willing to sit out there, propped on the ledge, until the dawn of a new age. Well, fine. Let him. At least then she didn't have to worry about waking up and finding his warm, *real* body anywhere near her. It was bad enough fighting the dreams that had been plaguing her in the weeks since Brett had reentered their lives without worrying about *that*. She could only hope that another room came available soon.

Finally, *finally,* the long day took its toll. Kate closed her eyes.

And slept.

Chapter Six

Stay in the too-small, too-hard chair, or stretch out on the floor?

Brett raked his fingers through his hair and considered his choices. Either way, he'd have to make do. That king-size mattress might have looked plenty wide during the cold light of day when they'd checked in, but now...in the dark, silent night, it seemed way too small.

He'd finally closed the balcony door against the noise of the occasional passing car. But he hadn't drawn the drapes against the moon and the cool white light drifted diagonally across the bed. Kate was a slender form under the sheet that she'd hitched tightly up under her chin. She hadn't moved a muscle in the past hour.

He knew, because he hadn't been able to drag his eyes from her.

The chair or the floor, he reminded himself.

Muttering an oath under his breath, he yanked off his shirt, pitching it in the corner, and went over to the air-conditioning controls to adjust the temperature a few degrees lower. Then he snatched the unused pillow from the bed, sat down in that infernal chair and balled the pillow behind his head. He'd long ago kicked off his shoes and he slumped down in the chair, propping his feet on the bed across from him, keeping well away from the narrow portion of mattress occupied by Kate.

He closed his eyes, willing sleep to come. His back protested his slouched position, but he ignored it just as he'd ignored it for years.

He'd ignored a lot of things for years.

The thought snuck in without permission and Brett pulled his feet from the bed and stood, moving restlessly around the room. He didn't dwell in what-might-have-beens. What the hell was the point?

His life was his own. He had his firm, a career that suited him right down to his boots. And in the occasional bit of time left over from that, he had friends to shoot hoops with and women to hit the sheets with.

A rustle from the bed drew his eyes.

Women to hit the sheets with. Yeah, right. Here he was in a room with Katy and he'd be pressed to remember the name of one of those women or how long it had been.

He shoved his fingers into his pockets, standing at the foot of the bed, watching her. It was almost as if she sensed it, for even in her sleep, she shifted again, almost protestingly. The sheet slipped downward. The flimsy strap of her pajama top had slipped down one shoulder. It was hard to tell in the dim white light from the moon, but it looked like the silky stuff was pink. Soft, pale pink.

She'd always gone for delicately colored pastel lingerie. She might wear black and red and royal-blue on the outside, but underneath she'd worn things as soft as spun sugar.

She made a low sound and the hair on his nape prickled.

He pulled his attention from that little strap draped over the beautiful curve of her arm to her face. Before he knew what he was doing, he'd moved around the side of the bed, going closer. Close enough to see the sheen of moisture on her forehead.

She mumbled and he frowned. The words were incoherent, but the strain in them came through loud and clear.

Aside from Caine, who'd never been much of a father to Kate—or to her brothers either, for that matter—and the lack of a mother, what did Kate have in her life that haunted her dreams?

She was wealthy, beautiful and young. Despite his occasional dig about her career, he knew she was making her mark in that area, as well. Yet here she was, tossing restlessly in her sleep. And crying out a brokenhearted "no, no, no."

He swore under his breath and sat on the side of the bed. "Kate. Wake up. You're having a nightmare."

His words had no effect. He settled his hand on her tensed arm. "Come on, Katy," he murmured. "Just breathe with me. It's only a dream."

She cried out, bolted upright, and stared blindly at him. "Don't leave me," she begged starkly.

He couldn't have been more startled if she'd faced him down with a shotgun. But even as his brain scrambled for coherency, she lay back, huddling against her pillow.

She was still asleep. He let out a long breath. Her hair was streaming over her face, and he reached out, smoothing it back. The strands felt like silk against his fingertips. He wanted to run his fingers deeply through it, and realizing it, he pulled his hand away.

Distance, he thought grimly. He needed distance from her. The more the better. Enough distance so he wasn't remembering the sexy underwear she liked. So he wasn't remembering the way it felt to have her hair slide through his fingers.

He almost wished the hotel *had* had another room that she could have used.

He pushed off the bed. It was getting close to dawn and he'd had zero sleep. Yeah, it would've been a hell of a lot easier if the hotel had had another room.

"Don't go."

What the hell was going on? "Kate—" He looked down at her, at the hand she'd wrapped around his wrist. But her eyes were closed. If she wasn't asleep, she was doing a good impression of it.

And if she wasn't asleep, she would never in a million years reach out for him.

Which meant she *was* asleep. Asleep and tormented by a dream that had her crying out loud.

He turned his wrist and caught her hand in his, frowning when her fingers slid against his, entwining. He didn't kid himself that she knew who she'd reached out for. Maybe she was thinking about Hamilton.

The thought gnawed at him. But not enough to untangle his fingers from hers. Not enough to walk away.

Swearing a blue streak in his mind, he sat down on the edge of the bed. Scooped her, tangled sheet and all toward the middle to make room for himself, and lay back.

She turned, snuggling the long line of her back against his side, still holding onto his hand.

At least the twanging ache in his back was happy now that he'd stretched out on the bed, he thought with grim humor. Even if the rest of his body had gone on red alert.

Then he heard her long sigh. It was one of relief. The sigh in his soul, however, was nowhere near as peaceful.

The warmth is what she noticed first.

The refreshment of having a decent night's sleep is what she noticed second.

She opened her eyes to the golden sunlight filling the room. It took a moment. Maybe a half a minute before it dawned on her that she wasn't in her own bedroom. Then reality sunk in.

The heat of a long, hard male body singeing her all down her back is what she noticed third.

Horror swept through her and she slid out from beneath the arm tucked over her waist and scrambled from the bed. She could hardly bring herself to look back at him. She could hardly prevent herself from doing so. And even as she watched, he rolled over until he was flat on his stomach, naked from the waist up, his back a strong stretch of darkly tanned satiny skin. His richly dark hair tousled around his head.

It was only the artist in her that made her fingertips tingle, she assured herself, and rapidly snatched up some clean clothes before shutting herself in the bathroom.

Every time she began to think about waking next to Brett Larson she hurried her motions to get rid of the thoughts. The result was probably the fastest shower on record.

She dried her hair using the blow-dryer provided by the hotel and scraped it back into a ponytail. She tried to put on some makeup, but her hands shook too badly so she ended up having to wash the blurred mascara off and start over.

Then she pulled on her red shorts and matching button-down shirt and buttoned it right up to the neck.

So what if she looked uptight and tense. She *was* uptight and tense. She'd just awakened with her backside tucked against Brett Larson.

It didn't matter that he'd been wearing jeans, that she'd been wearing her pink silk pajamas, or that there had been a sheet and blanket in between them.

The first opportunity she got, she was going to find herself another room, no matter *what* his objections were. She eyed herself in the mirror and nodded firmly. Her own room. It was absolutely imperative.

Straightening her shoulders, she pulled open the bathroom door and strode into the bedroom. Any vague hope that Brett might have still been sleeping died ignominiously at the sight of him sitting up on the bed. He'd mounded the pillows behind him, and the white bedding made him look even darker. He looked utterly masculine, utterly the king of his domain.

He looked like sin come to life, a little voice whispered inside her. And she couldn't refute it, either, she realized, as she dragged her attention upward from the unbuttoned waist of his jeans.

His heavy-lidded gaze rested on her and she had to fight the urge to fiddle with the cuffed hem of her cherry-red shorts.

"Sleep well?" He asked, one eyebrow peaking.

Her jaw tilted. "Yes. Just fine." Something in his

expression made her nervous and she impulsively reached over for the phone sitting on the bedside table.

''Who're you calling?''

''Home.'' She realized she was still eyeing his chest much too closely and hastily resumed dialing. ''I want to check on Daddy's condition.''

''Well, make it quick. I want to get an early start on the galleries as soon as we can after breakfast.''

''I want to get this job done as quickly as possible, too.''

''Getting tired of my company already?''

''Yes.''

His lip curled as he pushed off the bed and she jumped, scooting well out of the way. ''You didn't use to be so nervous the morning after.''

Her finger shook and she accidentally pushed the wrong button. She huffed and dialed over. ''This isn't the 'morning after.' Nothing happened in that bed but *sleep.*''

His teeth flashed for a moment and he drew one finger along her shoulder as he walked past her. ''You sure about that, Katy?''

Her mouth parted. She could hear the phone ringing in her hand and looked at it stupidly.

The rush of the shower began, clearly audible through the wall. She sat weakly on the edge of the mattress and wondered what kind of disaster she'd walked into this time.

Then she heard a voice on the phone and lifted it to her ear. ''Hello? Oh. Mrs. Hightower. Yes, of course. I know. I, uh, I called *you.*''

Half the day later, Brett looked down at Kate as she walked beside him. They'd already visited seven galleries and were on their way to the eighth. She was walking as if putting one foot in front of the other was a challenging act. "What's wrong with your feet?"

She didn't look at him. She'd managed *not* to look at him pretty much since they'd left the hotel that morning. "They hurt," she said.

He looked at the strappy little leather sandals on her feet. "Those boots aren't made for walking, princess."

"Had I been allowed more control over my packing," she said pointedly, "I would have been more appropriately outfitted. What's the name of the next gallery?"

He dragged his gaze from the length of her legs below the hem of her bright red shorts and looked at the list in his hand. "The Marissa Deane Gallery," he said. He looked up at the corner sign they'd just passed. "Should be on the next corner there. Then we'll catch a cab back to the hotel and you can put up your pretty little pampered feet."

She nudged her sunglasses up her nose and headed smartly down the sidewalk. But her walk was cautious and he felt like sludge. He'd pushed hard all day, wanting nothing more than to locate Madelyn LeClaire's dealer.

The effort had been a total bust, so far.

He knew it was early, considering the number of art dealers on his list, but he couldn't help wishing that once—just this once—they'd luck out with immediate success.

He wondered if Kate was mentally complaining as much as he was. If she was, she hid it better than he did. She hadn't complained about the hours they'd been hitting the pavement; she hadn't complained about the greasy spoon where they'd had lunch. Other than to silently wipe something off the seat of her chair before she sat down, she hadn't said much of anything, in fact.

When he thought about it, he knew it was damned uncharacteristic of the Kate Stockwell he knew.

They stopped for a traffic light, then crossed the street toward the next gallery. He could see the ritzy little sign hanging on the brick wall.

Whether her feet hurt or not, Kate's steps quickened and she reached the building first. Then Brett saw her shoulders droop. He joined her, and spotted the small printed sign in the corner of the plate-glass window. Closed for repairs.

He heard Kate sigh as she lightly tapped her fingernail against the window. "Well," she said evenly. "If we haven't found Madelyn's dealer by the end of the week, we can check back when this place is scheduled to be open again."

"Yeah." He hoped it wouldn't be necessary. That particular notion was beginning to stick in his head like a stuck record. He hailed a cab and hustled her inside. He gave the driver their hotel but Kate sat forward, countermanding the directions by telling the driver to take them to the nearest department store, instead. Then she glanced at him, clearly expecting a protest.

"I saw the way you were walking. Getting better shoes is only smart."

She shot him a cool blue look. "So that I won't slow you down even more?"

"I didn't say that."

Her eyebrow peaked. "You didn't have to. It's been screaming from your tall, silent self all day. I never would have pegged you for a sulky sort, Brett. Obviously I was wrong."

His laughter was short and amused. "Katy, you could

give lessons in the art of being sulky." He reached over and settled his finger on her soft lower lip, pressing down gently. Seeing her eyes flicker, startled at the touch. "You've had the art of pouting down to a fine science since you were fifteen. Pushing your lip out just this way when you weren't getting your way about something."

She deliberately lifted her chin and turned her head away from him. "So I was spoiled and pouting. You must count your lucky stars that you escaped a life sentence with someone like me."

"Thought we were leaving the past in the past."

"Don't look at me. You're as guilty of failing on that score as I am."

Since it was true, there wasn't much he could say. When the cab pulled up at the curb, Brett paid the fare and climbed out, stretching the kinks from his back. If he'd gotten more than an hour or two of sleep the night before, he might be in a better frame of mind, he knew. But since the reason for his sleeplessness was even now smoothing down her bright red shorts as she joined him on the sidewalk and wasn't likely to go away anytime soon, he seriously doubted when his next full night of sleep would be.

When he thought about it, he realized he hadn't had a decent night since he'd first met with the Stockwells and let himself in for this unexpected excursion down bad-memory lane.

They stepped through the sliding glass door and were instantly engulfed in the hushed, air-conditioned atmosphere. Kate, who clearly still possessed radar instincts when it came to shopping, immediately turned down one aisle and headed, unerringly, into the shoe department. Wishing he were just about anywhere else, Brett followed.

Resigned to a long wait while she explored the shoes, Brett found an empty, deeply cushioned chair and sat down. He idly picked up a pair of gold sandals from the display beside him and looked at the price tag.

Some things never change, he thought, and plunked the two-hundred-dollar shoe back on the glass shelf when Kate walked over to him. She wore thick, serviceable socks and white athletic shoes. He figured he was a bad case when he found the way those white socks were turned down in tidy cuffs around her slender ankles a sexy sight.

"Something wrong?" Her voice was artless.

She annoyed the hell out of him. She was sly and cunning and bore considerable watching. "You've gotten faster in your old age," he observed smoothly. "How many more pairs of new shoes you got in that bag?"

"None. And it gives me an uncommon amount of pleasure to remind you that if *I* am in my old age, then you're right there with me. A few months ahead of me, if we're going to be strictly accurate."

"By all means, let's be *strictly* accurate." He pushed out of the chair, unconsciously wincing at the pull in his back, and took the bag from her unresisting fingers. "When did you take the How To Shop In Less Than Fifteen Minutes course?"

"Probably around the time that you were graduating from the How To Lose Friends And Annoy People course. It's a good thing you have a staff of your own now, Brett. Otherwise you wouldn't be able to keep one client." She sailed out the door into the hot, humid afternoon.

He realized there was a grin on his face. Lack of sleep obviously affected him in odd ways.

He lengthened his stride and caught up with her outside the department store, then had to shorten it again in order to keep from passing her. Her shining ponytail bounced jauntily as she stopped at the corner and looked this way and that while they waited for the light to change.

He might needle her about getting older, but the truth of it was that she was more beautiful now than she'd been at eighteen. Her girlish prettiness had sharpened into finely patrician features. She had the kind of beauty that would never fade.

"What was the name of the next gallery on your list?"

The job. Concentrate on the job. "We've hit all the galleries on this particular stretch."

She peered at him as they crossed the street. "Are you sure? I thought there were more. You didn't bring the list?"

"No."

"Then how do you know? I thought you had a page from the list in your pocket."

"You want to argue about whether or not I'm carrying around a sheet from that list?"

"Well, no. It just seems to me that you can't possibly remember—"

"Next up is Gallery Blanding, Tallman Galleries, Sobleski Art and Pennington Design. Blandings is closest, but it closes in fifteen minutes and we're not gonna make it before then. Okay?"

The tip of her tongue peeped out and touched her soft lift. "You must have graduated from the School Of Better Memory, too.'' Her gaze skipped away from his, her smile taunting.

''Nice try, Katy,'' he murmured. The smile didn't fool him for a minute. He knew what she was thinking. ''Just because I used to get tied up with work and miss a date with you now and then because of it, didn't mean that I had a bad memory.''

''No.'' Again that smile that didn't cover some old emotion she'd probably deny feeling if he pointed it out to her. She turned sideways, letting a woman with a wooden push cart of fresh flowers pass by. ''It meant that I was further down the list of your priorities. And three times out of four isn't *now and then.*''

''You want me to apologize now for trying to get ahead back then?''

She shook her head, not answering, and quickened her step. Brett grimaced and lengthened his stride back to his natural gait. She couldn't outwalk him if she tried. She was too short in comparison to him. He reached out and curled his hand around her arm, bringing her up short. All around them, pedestrians walked, automobiles cruised and the August sun blazed down in all of its afternoon fury.

''Don't drop little fireballs and then expect me to ignore them, Katy. I'm not made that way.''

She shifted, her eyes meeting his for a long moment. An elderly couple brushed past them, giving them a stern look for blocking the sidewalk. ''I wish you wouldn't call me that.'' Her voice was stiff. ''It's not my name.''

''And I wish I could look at you without wanting to either strangle you or make love to you. Ain't gonna happen. Not for either one of us.''

Kate's mouth dropped open. If he'd wanted to shock

her, he couldn't have succeeded more thoroughly. He'd been needling her that morning with his "morning after" comment, but this…this was something entirely different. "Where did *that* come from? We both know that you're not pining over our…our lost relationship. You didn't eight years ago and you're certainly not doing so now!"

"Pining? Damn straight I didn't pine, sweetheart. Not after you turned around and raced down the aisle with my good buddy Hamilton."

"You didn't pine before that, either," Kate whispered. She couldn't believe what she was doing. Arguing. On a public street. If Brett had cared enough about her to pine *before* she'd married Hamilton, things might have turned out so very, very differently.

She was terribly aware of his hand on her arm and of the looks they were receiving. She began walking blindly in the direction of their hotel, feeling crowded and confined when he stuck right with her. "I'm sorry. This is just more awkward than I'd expected." She instinctively moved toward the curb, seeking to put some distance between them.

"Awkward's a pretty puny word, if you ask me," Brett said flatly. He wrapped his hand around her wrist, drawing her back toward the center of the sidewalk. "And I wish you'd have thought of that before you finagled your way here with me."

"I want to find Madelyn."

"Yeah. Bad enough that you're willing to endure my untrustworthy company in order to accomplish it."

Kate pressed her lips together. "All right," she said, appalled at the way her voice sounded hoarse and hurt. "That is exactly right," she forced the words out. "My need to find her is greater than my animosity for you."

"Hate."

Her teeth tortured the soft flesh of her inner lip. "I wish it were hate," she said painfully. "Then maybe this wouldn't be so difficult."

"This."

She waved her hand vaguely between them. "This. Being around you. Having to deal with you and knowing that you wish I were anywhere but here. I know my presence inconveniences you. You've made no secret of it."

"Is it just me, or are you just flat incapable of listening to anyone unless they're under five feet tall and covered in watercolor paint and modeling clay?

"You know nothing about my work," she flared.

"Sweetheart, you're a Stockwell. There's not a move you make that isn't of avid interest to the good folks of Grandview. And the fact that you seem to think you can ease the hearts and minds of your miniature patients by having them dabble their fingers in arts and crafts is one that causes a lot of talk."

Her shoulders were so stiff that a jostle from a passerby would have snapped her in two. "My work is *not* frivolous," she said frostily. "I have helped my patients and I won't stand here and let you degrade my—"

"I wasn't degrading anything," he cut her off, effectively removing the stung outrage from her sails. "Least of all your work. How the hell do you do it? Bounce from one topic to another, confuse the issue, hear meanings that aren't there and totally miss the meanings that are?"

Her professional pride settled around her like a familiar cloak. Shielding her against his intrusive gaze. Protecting her from the knowledge of her own failures. "I don't know what you're talking about."

"Do you give a straight answer to anything, anymore, Katy? Just say, flat out, what's on your mind?"

She shifted, uncomfortable. Impatient. "I really can't imagine what you're trying to get at here, Brett. You're annoyed that I insisted on coming with you to Boston. Though we'd like to, neither one of us seems quite able to eradicate an occasional mention of the past we, ah, shared. But that'll be fixed soon enough."

His eyebrow lifted, eyes and hair looking particularly dark and mocking against the white of his polo shirt. "How's that?"

"When I can get a separate room at the hotel. When we're not living in each other's pocket."

"Sometimes, Kate, you're like a stuck record. There are no rooms. No matter how often you flash your gold card, you're not going to get a room that doesn't exist. This town is full up. And even if you *did* go to another room, it doesn't erase the one thing that you seem determined to not hear me say!"

Her lips parted as his voice rose. As close to yelling as he'd ever gotten.

"The problem between us isn't your annoying habit of trying to control the world and everyone in it. It's the fact that things aren't finished between us."

Her eyebrows drew together, startled beyond words. "What?"

"We're not finished. Nothing was finished. Not even when you walked down the aisle with Ham." Brett stepped closer to her, stealing her breath and her resolve in one fell swoop.

His voice lowered. "Tell me, Katy. Was it good with him? As good as it was between us? Did you come apart in his arms the way you did in mine? Did you cry afterward because the emotions were so intense you couldn't help yourself?''

Kate flinched. She, above all people, understood the importance of closure. The value of catharsis. But having it occur on the teeming streets of Boston at that moment was devastating.

''Do you really want to know?'' she asked, her voice brittle. ''Or are you just trying to punish me for having had the nerve all those years ago to demand you agree to a wedding date, once and for all?

''You should have just told me right off that you didn't want to marry me when I proposed to you, Brett. It would've saved us all a lot of grief in the end. Instead you kept me dangling for two years. Just how long did you really think I would wait around until you *deigned* to marry me? Six more months? Six more years?'' She didn't want his answer. Rather, she didn't want to listen to his answer.

She turned and began walking down the sidewalk. Her movements felt stiff, uncoordinated. She felt relief and despair all rolled into a knot that threatened to choke her, when he didn't stop her.

But then, Brett had never stopped her. Not twelve years ago when, after that miserable argument in the hotel room where they were supposed to have shared their first time together—on the night of their prom, she'd stormed out and began walking home despite the late hour and her fragile heels.

Certainly not eight years ago when she'd impetuously invited Hamilton Orwell to dance at a wedding reception—when she'd been, for about the sixth time in one year, a bridesmaid—with the express purpose of making Brett jealous. He hadn't been jealous. He'd been coldly furious and contemptuous.

That had been the same day that their lives changed forever. When Kate finally had to admit to herself that Brett had meant it when he told her that if she wanted to set a date to get married, she could set a date with someone else.

Now, she told herself that she was glad that Brett didn't stop her from walking away from him. Being stopped by Brett Larson was no longer even a dot on her list of aspirations and dreams.

So why, then, did she feel desperately close to tears by the time she made it into the hotel's empty elevator? And why, when the gilded doors sighed shut, did she feel an emptiness inside her at the sight of him standing outside the car on the other side of the doors?

Chapter Seven

Brett stood in the elevator foyer and watched the doors slide closed, hiding the sight of Kate, huddling miserably against the wall.

He let out a sharp, fierce breath and rubbed his palm down his face. Day two and they were nearly ready for pistols at dawn. Going after her now would be his worst mistake since the mother of all mistakes he'd made in thinking he could get through even a few hours with Kate by his side and keep the past where it belonged...in the past.

He was disgusted. Where the hell was his control?

That was his claim to fame, after all. Brett Larson— the guy who never blinked, never flinched, never broke a sweat. Who never let anyone get under his skin. Not deadbeat dads, fugitives, felons, not seductresses who married and killed their husbands with reckless abandon, not even desperate mothers who disappeared with their children to save them from horrors too unspeak-able to mention. He was the guy who mopped up the tears of parents whose teenagers had run away; he was the guy who was used to dealing with *other* people's problems.

He was the guy who took on cases people figured couldn't be solved; the lost causes; the impossible odds. And more times than not, he beat the odds. Because he kept it under control.

Two days in Kate Stockwell's company and he was ready to lose it.

He wanted to throttle her, he wanted to shake her, he wanted to snatch her up against him and cover her mouth with his and slake the smoldering hunger for her that seemed destined to be his tormenting companion for life.

He turned on his heel and strode through the lobby.

He needed his head examined.

He needed a drink.

He pushed the flat of his hand against the smoked glass door that led into the lounge off one side of the lobby. Inside the lively bar, Happy Hour was in full force. The music was loud, cigarette smoke hung in the air, bodies crushed together, dancing on the small, square dance floor.

People stood, two and three deep at the curving high bar. It could have been a bar in any city in any state, in any country. God knows he'd spent enough time in them; not always following leads, either.

A cocktail waitress dressed in a skimpy uniform, cut low over a generous chest and high over gorgeous legs, appeared in front of him. He recognized the look in her eyes, the thought in her mind as her lashes lowered, taking stock of him.

And there'd been a time, after Kate, when he would have taken her up on the unspoken offer. When he had buried his heart and his emotions in one nameless woman after another. When he wasn't busy burying all that, he'd been busy drowning all that. In a bottle of bourbon. He wasn't proud of it. But he couldn't pretend that it hadn't occurred. And when he'd come out on the other side, he'd thought he'd left the emotions behind him.

He'd believed that until he'd picked up the phone one day to learn that the Stockwell family had a case they wanted him to consider.

Now, he looked at the waitress with her come-hither expression and felt nothing.

She wasn't brown haired and blue eyed and sleekly reserved in a wholly challenging way.

The cocktail waitress tilted her head and her long, auburn hair slid over her shoulder. "Sir?" Her lips caressed the word. "Can I get you some…thing?"

He didn't know what it was about him. He was just a guy. Too tall to fit comfortably in the coach section of an airplane, too wide in the shoulders to fit easily in off-the-rack suits. He remembered to cut his hair only when it started to hang in his eyes; mostly he shoved it back with one hand after he left his morning shower and the way it dried was the way it stayed.

But for some reason, women liked him. And he wasn't arguing with it. He was what he was.

And what he was, right now, was a man too close to the edge; too much in need of burying himself in a bottle. And because of it, he very deliberately shook his head and turned away from the waitress. Leaving the bar's noisiness and good-natured cheer behind in favor of the street and the rush-hour congestion there. He walked, deliberately shedding the emotion that clogged his senses. Emotion had never gotten him anywhere in the past. He didn't want it. Didn't need it. Feelings were wholly unwelcome, reminding him of things that weren't. That would never be.

By the time he stopped walking, it was nearing dark. How many bars had he passed? He'd lost count, not entering any of them. He'd gone by two more galleries, names that his memory had recorded the first time he'd seen the list prepared by his secretary. The galleries were both closed, but he tracked down the owners' nearby whereabouts; focusing on the task with deliberate single-mindedness. The legwork was second nature to him.

And finally, when he looked up to see what corner he'd managed to reach, he knew he could face a bottle of bourbon without wanting to crawl inside it and drink the memories back into the dim reaches of his mind where they didn't eat away at him. He started back, stopping only at a well-worn pub that served up the same cold beer and no-nonsense sandwiches that they'd had years before. They packed his order in a brown paper bag and he carried it with him as he went back to the hotel.

As he went back to Kate.

Kate heard the click of the door and stiffened, but refused to look up when it opened. She kept her eyes on the sketch pad propped against her knees. Brett entered and though she'd told herself she wouldn't, she nevertheless caught a glimpse of him. He looked weary and worn; as if he'd fought a battle he was still in danger of losing.

She swallowed the knot that rose in her throat. She

was imagining things. She refused to ask where he'd been all this time. She didn't want another confrontation with him. They'd already had too many.

His expression didn't change as he walked past the linen-covered skirted table that the room service folks had left, though he gave it a long, telling look. It was topped with silver domed dishes, a basket of fragrant rolls, a silver coffee pot, chilled wine and a single rose.

"I might've known," he muttered, finally looking from the display to Kate. He walked over to where she sat at the table with her feet propped on the edge of the bed opposite her and dumped a wrinkled paper bag on the table by her elbow.

Her nose picked up the scent of pickles and pastrami. "Is this for me?"

"I set it next to you, didn't I? Except, obviously, you were capable of taking care of yourself."

Her lips tightened. She'd spent so much time with her lips pursed since Brett had reentered her life that she had a vague fear they would never return to their normal shape. That Emma Hightower's cautions throughout Kate's childhood would run true—don't make faces, for what will you do if your face freezes that way? "Yes. It takes so much effort to pick up the phone and call room service," she said coolly. "And since you gave me no indication when you planned to return—" *if ever* "—I took care of it."

The fact that she'd dithered over the menu for nearly an hour, torturing herself with selecting the right dishes that might please him, was one she didn't intend to advertise.

"Between what I ordered and what you brought, you'll have a regular feast," she said as she reached for the sack. She pulled out the two paper-wrapped sandwiches and lay them out on the table, then withdrew a sweating bottle of root beer and a foam cup filled with a melting frozen lemonade.

She stared at the confection, at once forgetting about the room service tray laden with the chilled salads she'd ordered, the iced shrimp, the petits fours.

Oh, Brett. What are we doing here?

He'd bought her a frozen lemonade on their first "official" date when they were sixteen years old. They'd shared it, eating with the same spoon, drinking it with the same straw when it melted so much that it was more a beverage than a dessert. And after he'd pushed the cup into the trash can at the park where they'd been picnicking, he'd closed his hands over her shoulders and drew her up onto her toes to meet his lips.

Even at sixteen he'd been tall, more gangly than he'd liked; but within a year he'd caught up with his height as his chest had begun to fill in with the makings of the man to come. He'd tasted of lemonade.

And despite the fact that she'd thought him impervious to nerves, even way back then, his hands had been shaking when they closed over her shoulders.

That was the day that she'd known she loved him.

She'd just known.

"Got a bug in the drink or something?"

Kate dragged her thoughts from the futile past and shook her head. "No. It's…it's fine."

He nodded once, but didn't sit. He picked up the sandwich and the soda and moved out onto the balcony, as if he couldn't bear to remain enclosed in the same room with her.

He was leaning over the edge of the balcony, his shirt stretching tightly between his shoulders, then gathering in sharply down his long back, disappearing into his jeans. As she watched, he tilted the bottle to his lips with an economical movement, causing muscles to flex beneath the blindingly white fabric.

She forced herself to eat at least part of the sandwich more because she knew she had to than because she had any appetite left. She uncovered one of the beautifully presented shrimp cocktails and carried it out to him, handing the crystal container to him.

She wasn't at all sure that he'd take it. His expression seemed completely unwelcoming. But then he reached for it with a grunt of thanks. Kate watched him select a shrimp, sink his teeth into it and turned on her heel, nearly tripping in her haste to get off the balcony.

She headed back to her chair-perch and her sketch pad. The lemonade sat in the middle of the table. Slowly the level of the frozen drink lowered, collapsed as it continued to warm. To melt.

Kate looked away from it finally and began moving her hands over the sketch pad. She was just flipping the page filled with too many distressing images to a fresh one when Brett came back inside.

"Just to get something straight," he said expressionlessly, "I'm not pining over you."

Her brows pulled together. "I know."

"Make sure you do. When I said we weren't finished, I wasn't talking about emotionally."

Her eyes narrowed. Across the top of her sketch pad, both her hands toyed with the thick drawing pencil. "Really."

"Just so we're clear."

"Clear," she repeated faintly.

"Good. We're agreed then."

She tucked her tongue for a moment against her teeth. "On what...exactly?"

"That the only thing unfinished between us is the sex."

Her half-amused, half-annoyed state fled. Her skin suddenly felt hot and itchy and much too tight. "Sorry to disappoint you, Brett—" her tone said she was anything but sorry "—but sex *is* definitely finished between us." She deliberately looked back at her sketch pad. "It is a nonissue."

"Why? Because you say it is? Well, of course. Why didn't I figure that out? God knows that whatever Katy Stockwell says goes."

She ignored his caustic words. Continued moving her pencil across the white sheet, her movements jerky and furious. Then her hand stopped, not knowing what stroke of the pencil to make next. It was as frustrating as opening your mouth to speak, only to suddenly find the words had run out on you when your back was turned.

For Kate, her sketching had always been her outlet. And now, *he* was messing with that, too. She slapped the pencil down on the table and slammed shut her sketch book. "If everything I said became a reality, I wouldn't be cooped up in this room with you!"

His eyes, dark and unreadable, roved over her. "Yeah. Cooped up. I came in with those sandwiches what…thirty minutes ago? Forty-five at the most. How you gonna feel after another twenty-four hours? You should go back to Grandview, Kate. I'll find Madelyn for you. You can trust me that far."

She hopped out of the chair. "No! I'm not going to go toddling off home just so you can sleep easier with me gone."

Brett watched her steadily. "*I* sleep fine, Katy-did. You're the one troubled with nightmares."

Her mouth parted, as if prepared to fire off another round, but his words sank in and she just stood there. Soft lips parted, as if they were waiting for a kiss. Eyes widened as if they were waiting for something.

Then her expression smoothed. Her lips pressed together, firming. Making him want to kiss them back to that soft, yearning state. ''I don't know *what* you mean,'' she said.

Airy. Snooty. Just a hint of arrogance, and a whole passel of challenge.

It had the same effect it had always had.

Brett cursed inwardly. He was a man through and through. And some things didn't change. He was taking a step toward her before he could stop himself. And another.

Seeing her eyes, those beautiful blue eyes, flicker for a moment, then meet his head-on.

Oh, yeah. Definitely challenging.

And it suddenly wasn't about the past at all.

It was about the two of them. Right here. Right now.

Man. Woman.

Alone.

Feeling a hot pulse flowing in his bloodstream like some kind of heady, unavoidable beat, he reached for her. Saw the way her eyes flashed, the way her expression went from contrary to vulnerable and back again.

And then she was in his arms. Mouth against his. All hot and flash and fire. Her head fell back over his arm, her arms, slender and infinitely strong, twined around his shoulders, sinking into his muscles. He felt her shudder, her mouth opening, and drove ever deeper. Wanting to absorb her. Wanting to imprint his soul on hers, and hers on his.

She tasted of tart lemonade and liquid warmth. And

he couldn't get enough of it. His hands swept down her spine, feeling every small nubby ridge, sliding out over the swell of her hips in her taunting red shorts, up to her waist; narrow and slender. His fingers spread and his thumbs brushed the outer swell of her breasts and she trembled wildly against him.

He did it again and she moaned, deep into his mouth, where their breaths meshed and merged and he couldn't tell where he ended and she began.

Satisfaction roared through him that she was here, where she belonged. Finally back where she belonged—

W-h-o-a.

Brett jerked up his head and let her loose so abruptly that she wavered and plopped inelegantly onto the corner of the bed. He had to grab her before she slid right off onto the floor.

Her cheeks were flushed, her eyes were blue flame. She shoved at his hands, yanking out of his reach. "Leave me alone! How...how *dare* you!"

"Dare?" His fingers on his hips, he looked at her. "You had your fingers in my hair, Katy. Your tongue down my throat."

She turned even more fiery red. "I did not."

His lip curled. "Right."

Her nostrils flared delicately. Like a racehorse prepared for flight. Sleek and beautiful, delicate and powerful. "I detest you."

"Yeah, but you *want* me."

Her breasts rose and fell. Drawing his gaze to the full swell of them against her blouse. He thought, for a long, tense moment, that she was going to deny it.

That she'd pretend nothing was happening.

That she'd refuse, rebut and retreat the way she'd done so many times in the past. But she didn't.

And Brett damned himself for feeling another curl of need wend its hypnotic way through his blood. He didn't want to admire her passionate temper; her headstrong ways. It was those things that had contributed to the misery of the past.

But she didn't fly into a tearful tantrum. She didn't issue ultimatums that she'd had to have known he wouldn't bow to.

She gathered herself up, tall and straight and so ungodly desirable that it was sinful in someone so elegant. She looked down her nose at him, despite the fact that he towered more than a half foot over her.

"I may want you," she allowed. Her voice was cool. The kind of cool that challenged a man to warm it up. "But that's where it will stay. I'm here in Boston for one purpose only. To find Madelyn. All the rest is..." For the first time, her eyes filled with something he couldn't identify. Something he couldn't name.

Something racked with pain; the kind of pain that could make a woman cry out in her nightmares.

His eyes narrowed. "Is...?"

Right before his very eyes, her expression smoothed once more. "Is useless," she said flatly. "Purely and simply useless. So if you're looking for a bedmate, look elsewhere. I'm not playing. I'm sure you won't have trouble finding one. In fact, I believe I heard that Donna Lee Delatore moved to Boston not long after she got her degree. Look her up. She couldn't keep her claws off you when you and I were engaged. She rented the apartment next door to us just so she could be close to you. I'm sure she'd still be more than willing to play since you're oh-so-eligible."

Donna Lee Delatore. Now that *was* about the past. And it was definitely a hit below the belt. "You never believed that there was nothing going on between Donna and me.''

Kate lifted one shoulder. ''Whether there was or not is hardly of any interest to me now.''

''The first time I was within a foot of Donna Lee was at Jody and Russell's wedding reception. And I was dancing with *her* only because you were hell-bent on having another argument about setting a wedding date and I wasn't in the mood for it.''

''You certainly looked in the mood for Donna Lee.''

He watched her. ''Not anywhere as much as you did when you turned around and started dancing with Ham.''

''I only danced with Hamilton because you were humiliating me in front of all our friends by getting into a clinch with Donna Lee!''

''A few dances in a crowded wedding reception don't mean squat, Kate. Now you, you turned around and married Hamilton.''

Her lashes swept down, color receding from her cheeks. ''That was different.''

His oath was terse and to the point. ''What made it different? The fact that you ended up married made it okay that you were two-timing me with him?''

Her jaw dropped. ''I was not!''

''Yeah. Right.''

''Brett, I didn't have *any*thing to do with Hamilton until after the—'' She broke off, suddenly. As if even she didn't want to bring it up.

But he knew.

''Until after the car accident,'' Brett finished for her. The car accident that had left him with a back that hated humidity and rain. The car accident that had ruined her aspirations of becoming an artist. The car accident that—had they not been arguing after that miserable wedding reception when everything between him and Kate had seemed to explode—he should have been able to avoid.

Instead they'd both ended up in the hospital. And when Brett had finally managed to get to her room, it had been to find Caine Stockwell standing in the door, sneering down at him like he wasn't fit to wipe his shoes. And when Caine handed back the engagement ring that Brett had given Kate—the ring she'd sworn she'd never remove—he'd known it was over.

Over. Done. Finished.

He *had* wanted to wait to get married so that his business was more settled, so that he could provide for his passionate, beautiful Kate who had been his best friend since they were little more than kids.

They'd had all the time in the world, he'd thought.

They were together. They would make it to the church eventually, for their own wedding.

But that night, at Jody and Russell's wedding reception, Kate had seemed to hit the limit. He still didn't know what had set her off.

And, Brett supposed, these eight years later, it didn't matter a hill of beans in the scheme of things.

His reasons were more or less the same as hers. He was in Boston for one reason and one reason only.

To find Madelyn Johnson Stockwell LeClaire.

It was high time he remembered it.

Chapter Eight

"I'd just as soon not talk about the accident," Kate said carefully into the thick, tense silence. She couldn't bear to look at Brett. Not after having thrown herself into his arms like some raving, desperately lonely woman.

"Yeah, well, it's not my favorite subject, either," Brett muttered, shoving back his hair. His gaze rested on her, dark and unreadable. A muscle twitched in his jaw. "But it's kind of like having that proverbial elephant sitting in the living room and trying to pretend it's not there."

"I am not pretending the accident didn't happen," Kate told him stiffly. Good Lord, how could she? Her entire life had changed as a result of it. "I just don't see any point in discussing it with you."

His lips thinned and his eyes hardened into impervious chips of frozen chocolate. "And since the mighty

Kate Stockwell has spoken, the rest of the lesser mortals should just acquiesce.''

Pain swept through her. ''Am I such a witch, Brett?'' Tears burned behind her eyes, but she refused to give into them. ''Did our...split...ruin your life? Did it keep you from achieving everything you'd ever wanted in your life?''

She smiled humorlessly, lifting one hand expressively toward him. ''You're exactly where you wanted to be. You're the man you envisioned when you were only fifteen years old. You're successful and in control of your own destiny. And you did it all on your own, just like you knew you would. The accident happened. We were over. And you went on. So why can't we just forget about it and move on?''

''Can you forget, Kate?''

There were so many things in her life that she couldn't forget, not the least of which was Brett. There wasn't one moment of their friendship, then their love, that she couldn't recall with a clarity that never failed to bring her pain.

''I moved on,'' she lied.

''But did you forget?''

She stared at him, wishing the words to come. Hating that they wouldn't.

''You didn't forget about the accident. Not about what happened before or after,'' he continued in a low, flat voice. ''Any more than I did. That night—''

''—was a long time ago.'' She couldn't bear it another second. Not standing here, talking about the night he'd broken her heart. When she'd finally had to acknowledge that he'd walked away from her. For good. ''It's in the past and that's where it'll stay.''

His lips twisted. ''Since I agree with you, there

shouldn't be anything for us to argue over, should there?''

Kate's teeth were in danger of chewing through her inner lip. She drew in a sharp breath. Brushed her hands down her shorts, smoothing them. ''I think I'll go down to the lounge. For a while.''

''Why?''

So I can get away from you for a while. So I can breathe again. ''Change of scene,'' she said evenly.

''I'll go with you.''

''No!''

His eyebrow peaked.

''I mean, I—'' She broke off, not knowing what she meant. She hated it that this man, only this man, could make her brain fog, could make her dizzy and breathless and so incredibly weak and stupid.

She realized she was looking at the cup of melting lemonade. ''Why do *you* want to go with me, Brett?'' Turning the question around was only slightly satisfying. She didn't expect him to answer.

And when he did, her surprise reminded her that she knew very little about the man he was now.

''Because I don't want to think about you going to that bar and having some strange guy coming over and hitting on you.''

She absorbed that. ''Men don't pick me up in bars,'' she finally said.

Brett snorted softly. ''Only because you freeze them in place at fifty paces, sweetheart.''

She flinched, and hated it. ''So I am bossy and arrogant and cold. Well, thank you, Brett. This has been enlightening.'' The words came out without thought. Flippant. And every bit as chilly as he'd just condemned. She stepped past him, reaching jerkily for her purse and heading for the door.

"I don't want you going down there alone."

Kate couldn't look at him. "Well, sometimes we don't get what we want, do we?" She reached for the door. Coming with him to Boston had been an enormous mistake.

Enormous.

Her brothers trusted Brett to solve the mystery of Madelyn's whereabouts. And she didn't *not* trust him, no matter what he thought. She simply should have found another way to feel useful, because she'd obviously been fooling herself in thinking that she could coexist with Brett on any level.

His hand reached out as she passed and wrapped around her elbow, stopping her short. He stood over her, tall and broad and intense. "What you are, Kate—" his voice was low and deliberate "—is headstrong and passionate and wary. It's a killer combination, sweetheart. If I was worried about what I really wanted, you and I wouldn't be standing here, circling each other like wary lions. We'd have shut off our minds and we'd be having sex." His gaze flicked to the bed. "Right there. Right now."

How could she be shocked by him? Yet she was. And it rooted her to the floor. "You're even more impossibly egotistical than you used to be if you think you can just snap your fingers and I'll fall into your arms." Fiery heat raced through her cheeks. Not only had she awakened that morning in his arms, but "fall" into his arms is just what she'd done not five minutes earlier.

"You don't want to put that to the test, Katy."

Her temper, too close to the surface, where her nerves were already frayed and shot, gurgled. Bubbled perilously close to the edge. It didn't matter that he was right. That she was very much afraid she would try to climb right inside his skin if he so much as looked at her crookedly. "And you don't want to tell me what to do," she warned.

A light in his eyes flared. Around her arm, his fingers slowly flexed and every nerve in her body went on alert. A muscle leaped in his jaw. She felt breathless. On the edge of a deep, dark precipice.

Then control slowly inched over him. The tension left his hold on her elbow. His face smoothed into impassive lines. And in his eyes—oh, his dark chocolate eyes—it was as if he'd pulled down a window shade, hiding his thoughts and his soul from her.

She didn't know whether to laugh or cry. Whether to stay, or run. And it had been eight years since she'd felt so off balance. So out of kilter. He maddened her, purely and simply.

She knew it was altogether wiser and safer to leave. To resist poking at that sleeping dog any more than she—than he—already had. For a woman who helped others deal with their emotions, she was doing a miserable job of helping herself.

Wise and safe hadn't brought her to Boston. It hadn't cooped her up in this hotel room with Brett.

She deliberately pulled her elbow from his hold and set down her purse. She walked over to the table, feeling Brett's gaze following her, and picked up the lemonade dessert-drink. She carried it past him, past the room service cart, into the spacious bathroom where she upended it, pouring the contents right down the drain.

She rinsed the sink, walked back, looked at him and tossed the cup into the narrow trash can sitting on the floor next to the dresser. Right behind him.

"You throwing down a gauntlet, Katy?" His words were so soft they might have been a lover's whisper and she knew without question that he'd bought the lemonade deliberately. That he remembered their first "official" date just as well as she.

Her blood coursed through her veins. She was playing with fire. She knew it. He knew it.

If she was smart, she'd give in first. She'd capitulate. If she was smart.

Unfortunately Kate was beginning to suspect she was a raving lunatic. And backing down from Brett Larson was something she'd never been able to do with any semblance of regularity.

"What if I am?" Her voice was smooth. Masking the fact that she was just one enormous mass of jitters. "What are you going to do, Brett? What can you possibly do?"

"Other than send your sweet behind back to Texas?"

She didn't believe he would do that. Not anymore. If she was going to return to Texas before they found the answers they sought, it was going to be her own choice that sent her there. Her own choice, or her own fear.

She stared at him. Excruciatingly aware of him. And painfully aware that the man who so fascinated her was *this* man. Not necessarily the memory of the boy who'd been her first love.

"Other than send me back to Texas," she agreed, slowly. "You don't control me, Brett."

"Nobody ever did, that's for damn sure."

"And if I want to go down to the bar and pick up twenty men, it is nobody's business but my own."

"It is if you're figuring on bringing your football team back up to this room. I'm surprised, though, Kate. Always figured you were more discriminating."

As far as she was concerned, if he figured she'd had a multitude of lovers, that was fine. While he was thinking that, he wouldn't be figuring out that she'd had only two lovers in her life.

Hamilton Orwell; the man she'd foolishly married.

And Brett Larson; the man she'd foolishly loved.

She stared at him, tension arcing between them.

Then nearly jumped out of her skin, when the phone bleated. She blinked. Watched stupidly as Brett, smooth as molasses, turned to the phone and picked it up. Spoke. Then held it out toward Kate. "It's Jack."

Kate's stomach clutched in an entirely new way. She'd spoken with Rafe that morning, so why was Jack calling now? She snatched the phone and held it to her ear. "Jack? Is Daddy—"

"He's still hanging tight, kiddo, but the doctors say it probably won't be long." Jack's voice sounded far away, but grim.

Even knowing the end was coming, the news was still hard to take. Kate swallowed. "How are *you* doing? Maybe I should come home, after all." Of all of them, Caine had been hardest on Jack. She knew he'd returned to Grandview out of duty and family honor rather than because he'd been devastated over Caine's terminal illness.

"You coming home won't change anything with the old man. The only person he tolerates around him is Gunderson." Jack had never much been one to bare his feelings, so Kate wasn't surprised that he didn't tell her how he, himself, was feeling. "I've been looking into finding descendants on the Johnson side of the family," he continued. "Only ones I've been able to trace are a boy and girl who live on a farm near Tyler with their widowed mother."

"So you think the letters we found in Daddy's things are true? That the land where the Stockwells had their first oil strike was actually swindled from the Johnsons years earlier?" Her brothers had been trying to verify the accuracy of the accusation for weeks, to no avail.

"I'm not ruling anything out," Jack said shortly. "I'm thinking of heading that way and looking into things. Truthfully, though—" his voice gentled a few degrees "—the main reason why I was calling was to check on how *you're* doing."

Kate felt a sudden, fresh wave of heat fill her cheeks. Aware of Brett standing right there, clearly planning to listen in, she turned her back on him and sat down on the edge of the bed.

"Kate?" Jack asked again.

"Fine," she finally managed to say. "Just peachy," she added, deliberately cheerful.

Brett finally stopped watching her and turned to the room service cart to push it outside into the hall, then moved over to his computer that sat on the dresser. Kate closed her eyes for a moment, holding the phone to her ear.

"Didn't sound real convincing, kiddo."

She glanced over, only to find that Brett wasn't paying her a drab of attention. She turned around again, holding the phone to her ear. "I'm okay, Jack. It's just...more difficult than I expected."

The silence that met her on the other end was telling. And she moistened her lips. The only one who knew the entire story of her breakup with Brett was her big brother, Jack. She heard him sigh quietly. "How's the search going?"

So she told him about the galleries they'd visited.

"Nothing to shout over," she finished. "Hopefully we'll make more headway in the morning."

"And what are you doing now, in the evening?"

Kate flushed. Driving each other to madness. She cleared the knot from her throat. "Brett's working on his computer, and I'm sketching." It was more or less the truth and she didn't feel any need to confess all to Jack.

"But you *are* doing okay," he pressed.

She couldn't help the faint smile that formed. "Yes."

"Good. I like Brett. Always did. I'd hate to have to hustle to Boston to kick his caseload if he's—"

"He's not," Kate said hurriedly, torn between amusement and tears. She asked about the rest of the family, to distract him, and it worked.

Only because Jack allowed it to work, she knew. Her brother, so still and quiet and controlled. There was so much that she wished for him. That she feared he'd never open himself up to experience.

And a few minutes later, she was replacing the receiver.

She could hear the soft click of the computer keys beneath Brett's fingers. The passing traffic outside and below the open balcony door.

Mostly what she heard was the pulse of her own heart, beating in her head.

She rose, moistened her lips and turned to look at Brett. His fingers paused over his puny-looking keyboard as he looked at her.

She may have tossed down a gauntlet, but now she was afraid to acknowledge it. Afraid to pick it up. Afraid to kick it away.

The past hovered between them like a ghostly specter.

The present was curling around them like a seductive thief.

And the gauntlet lay between them.

Untouched.

Chapter Nine

Kate stared at the gallery clerk, trying hard not to let excitement rid her of her common sense, but they'd just received the first real indication that even one single painting of Madelyn LeClaire's had passed through Boston.

Beside her, Brett was smiling, dark and sexily charming as he slid his arm around Kate's shoulder, his fingers seeming to absently smooth back and forth over the ice-green spaghetti strap of her lightweight sundress.

She immediately hunched, annoyance flooding through her. "Brett—"

He cast a doting look her way, then returned his attention to the clerk. "My bride is anxious to find another LeClaire," he murmured indulgently. "I'm sure if you looked, you'd find the name of the buyer for the painting you're thinking of."

The girl's brown eyes were glued to Brett. "Oh, that

is *so* romantic,'' she gushed. ''But the owner, Mr. Maldovan, is on a buying trip and I don't have access to that information. He'll be back tomorrow morning, though, if you want to check back.''

''If you hear from him before then, would you mind giving him our number?'' Brett smiled and the clerk beamed, agreeing immediately.

Kate very nearly rolled her eyes, wishing she could look away, but not quite able to make herself do so. Particularly when Brett reached across and drew out the pen the clerk had tucked through her skeins of white-blond hair, to scrawl his name and their hotel number on a small square of paper that he pulled from the neat stack behind the small desk situated in the rear of the gallery. He smiled his thanks at the clerk and as she and Brett left the gallery, Kate wondered why the girl hadn't just dissolved in a puddle.

''I *told* you that we needed to check out this place! Is this it?'' she asked as soon as they left the cool interior behind for the hot afternoon. ''Our break?''

Brett looked down at Kate's glowing face. Her hair was piled on top of her head in an intriguingly rumpled mess, and her skin looked golden and silky against the shimmering green dress she wore. Hardly even green, he thought. More like a gloss of winter frost over a summer lime.

Then he realized what his thoughts had formed and swallowed an oath. So now he was getting poetic? It wasn't bad enough that he'd spent most of the last two nights restlessly watching Kate sleep? That the bags under his eyes had bags because he was awake and waiting for that moment that seemed to occur each night in the early hours when Kate started to toss and turn and moan protestingly.

When she did, he'd move stiffly from the side chair and lay down beside her. He'd brush her hair back from her heated face. And she'd calm. And sleep.

Leaving him even more sleepless.

And because of it, he was deriving a hell of a lot more pleasure out of needling Kate than was wise considering the way she'd pretty well declared a duel with her actions with the frozen lemonade.

He still didn't know what stupidity had pushed him into purchasing that lemonade in the first place. But he'd seen the little stand. Thought of his and Kate's first date.

And that had been all she wrote.

Now, standing on the sidewalk outside of Maldovan's Gallery, he thumbed his sunglasses into place. Then he smoothly dropped his arm over her shoulder, well aware of the way she subtly shifted and shrugged and tried to move away. "Is this our break?" He focused on her question. "Might be. Might not be." Somehow or other, his fingertips had found their way beneath the silky cord of a strap over her shoulder.

She snatched it back into place, fairly doing a shimmy to step out from beneath his arm. She pushed her own sunglasses in place. "Well," she said, a bit defiant, a bit breathless, "I think this is our break. You're just downplaying it because you'd crossed this place off your list of possibilities."

"They handle modern art, exclusively."

"Very *expensive* modern art, and some of Madelyn's pottery was definitely modern."

Amusement curled inside Brett. She was right in that he'd removed Maldovan's from the list of galleries to visit. How she'd settled on this one place, when she'd been paging through his list and notes, he'd never know.

And he'd visited the place more as a means of placating her than anything else. But it was hard to not feel some of her tense excitement rubbing off on him despite the years of experience that had jaded him. "Just don't be too disappointed if it isn't."

"I won't," she said confidently.

And he swore under his breath again. That confident, edgy excitement was bound to deflate sooner or later. It concerned him only because he was going to be the schmuck who had to pick up the pieces when her bubble *did* get jabbed with a sharp point. "I'll remind you of that," he muttered.

Her eyebrow lifted slightly. "Crab."

"Brat."

He figured on an icy look. A high-and-mighty Katy Stockwell glare.

What he got, however, was a grin, then a laugh. Musical and rich and full. The first full-fledged laugh he'd heard from her lips in eight long, long years. And the pendulum of his feelings toward her slammed into one heavy dark corner of pure, inescapable want.

Right there on a bloody sidewalk in Boston.

Kate had already turned and was walking along the sidewalk. The skirt of her dress swirling and swaying around her thighs. The stuff was so light, so airy that it seemed almost as if she were walking along in her own little cloud of iced-over green.

He supposed it ought to have looked odd that below her very feminine dress, her long, lightly tanned legs ended in her white athletic shoes. But on Kate, it seemed to fit. She looked young and vibrant and sexy as hell.

A breeze drifted through, lifting the hem and he waited…smiling to himself when her hand absently smoothed down the fabric before it could drift any higher than the middle of her thighs.

He shoved his hands into his pockets and followed her. He'd always been a sucker for a great set of legs.

And Kate's were still world class.

He cursed.

Kate was pulling ahead, and Brett wondered for a moment what she was in such a hurry for, but then he saw the hot dog peddler situated at the corner of a little green park that looked as if it had been plunked down in the middle of the busy neighborhood for no reason whatsoever.

She was ordering when he joined her.

And he was so surprised that he nearly commented on it. It had been pretty obvious since he'd come back into Kate Stockwell's world that she didn't eat enough. And since she was as thin as she could be without looking unhealthy, he figured her lack of appetite had more to do with stress than vanity.

He shook his head when the vendor looked at him; pulled out some cash and paid for the lunch, ignoring the fact that Kate had been prepared to pay for it herself. Then he watched her studiously apply a perfect drizzle of ketchup to the hot dog. He exhaled roughly and turned abruptly to purchase a long, tall bottle of icy water from the vendor, after all.

He could use the icy water for a makeshift shower, he thought wryly, and dragged his eyes from the way Kate was diligently preparing her food. And then it was a walk over to a bench in the shade and another bout of pretending he was oblivious to the way she ate.

Enthusiastically.

As if she hadn't eaten in days.

Well, as far as he was concerned, she hadn't much

eaten in days. If she ate a dozen hot dogs, he'd have sat there and waited.

He sat down beside her, stretching out his legs. Twisting open the cap of his water. "Not exactly a five-star restaurant." He lifted the water bottle and poured some down his throat.

"I've eaten in many five-star restaurants," Kate dismissed.

Brett stared into the narrow mouth of the water bottle. Every time he went into one of those fancy places, he wondered whether he was using the correct fork. "With Hamilton, no doubt."

He felt her gaze, then she shrugged a little. "Sometimes," she allowed evenly. "We were married for four years. We had to eat somewhere."

Again, Brett felt her gaze.

"Seeing how I'm still a miserable cook," she added smoothly.

Brett shook his head, glancing her way, catching the unexpected glint of humor in her eyes. "You were pretty bad."

"You were worse," she countered mildly. "Between the two of us, we couldn't butter bread without burning down the apartment."

She lifted her foil-wrapped dog. "Five-star restaurants have their place in the world. But this, well, this is a little bit of heaven." She bit into it, making a soft little humming sound of delight.

Brett pushed from the bench and chugged the water. He wasn't a kid, anymore. So why was he feeling as if he was nineteen again—staying in that postage stamp of an apartment with her—when everything she did and said put him in a state of near pain?

There was no way that Katy knew what effect she

was having on him. Despite the "gauntlet" that they'd both been pretending hadn't been tossed down between them, he could see by the smooth, clear expression on her face that she just didn't have a clue.

When he turned around again, she had finished her hot dog and was wiping her lips and fingers with all the elegance anyone could muster while using a ketchup-and-mustard-anointed paper napkin. She balled up her trash in her hand and the paper and foil bundle crinkled. "Do you think our chances of finding Madelyn this quickly are good?"

God, he hoped so. "Anything is possible, Kate," he said calmly. "We'll know when we talk to Maldovan."

She spread her fingers flat and looked down at the crumpled foil and paper in her hand. "I'm sorry that I made you think I didn't trust you to do your best on this case."

He looked at her. At the gleam of sunshine caught in the silky strands of rich brown hair. "You didn't trust me."

She shook her head slightly. "I've always known how dedicated you are. But I would have said just about anything to be a part of this search."

"You want to find her pretty badly. That's understandable."

"I needed to do my part. But, when it comes right down to it, I'm afraid to find her," she admitted in a soft voice.

That surprised him. "Why?"

She didn't answer. Not right away. And Brett wasn't sure, then, that she would. It wasn't as if they'd made a habit lately of soul-baring confessions. She slowly passed the crumpled ball from one hand to the other.

"Did you ever wonder about your father, Brett? You never used to talk about him much."

It wasn't the answer he'd expected. Trust Kate to ask a question of her own in place of answering. His stock answer, *Hell no,* was on the tip of his tongue when he realized that she was looking up at him. Honest curiosity filling her eyes. "I wondered a lot about him when I was a kid," he admitted.

"But not now?"

His shoulders moved, the back of his neck feeling twitchy. "I know what matters. He got my mother pregnant and hit the road."

Her eyes shifted. She seemed to find an inordinate amount of interest in the ball of paper she held. "Do you hate him?"

Brett exhaled and sat back down on the bench beside her. "Are you saying you hate your mother, Katy?"

"No!" Her blue gaze flew to him. "No, of course not."

"Then what is this about?"

She looked down again. The fine line of her jaw worked for a moment and he started to reach for her, barely curtailing the motion when she lifted her head again and her eyes met his. "I don't know," she whispered, pain written on her face. "I'm a therapist, for God's sake. Why can't I decipher my own emotions?"

At that, Brett did reach for her, wiser sense be damned. "Hell, Katy, it's a lot easier to see things when you're not personally involved. You oughta know that better than anyone."

Kate sighed, pressing her forehead to Brett's shoulder. She could hardly bear it that she found comfort in his arms. Not with all that had passed between them, all the bad feelings, the wrenching pain, the heartbreak.

Yet, her hands found their way to his chest as if they'd finally gone home.

And she couldn't make herself move away, even though she knew it would be much smarter to do so. Even though they were right out there on a public street in a public park on a public bench. "I can't forget that she may not want to be found."

Brett's hand closed around her neck and he tucked her head beneath his chin. "I shouldn't have told you that."

"Why not? It could well be true."

"It could just as easily not be true. Don't worry so much about things you can't control. We'll find Madelyn. And you'll get the answers you need."

"That painting has to be of my sister. It has to be, Brett. She couldn't be much more than a year younger than I."

His silence spoke volumes.

Kate knew that, even now, Brett carried a snapshot of that painting of the brown-haired girl in his pocket. He'd shown it to a hundred people by now and each time Kate saw it, it needlessly reminded her of the love that had been imbued in the painting. She was an artist herself, but even the most unartistic person on the planet would be able to see the love that had accompanied each and every brushstroke.

A mother's love.

"I don't even know my own sister's name."

Brett's hand stroked her hair. And it was so comforting, so tender, that it broke her heart. She scooted back, away, and felt chilled when his arms slowly fell from her, even though the afternoon was hot and humid.

She was a Stockwell.

Weakness was not an option.

"You will know it," Brett said.

"Maybe you're better off not knowing who your father is," Kate said. "What if he'd been anything like Caine?"

"I didn't say I didn't know who he was."

Kate stared. All thoughts slid away at the statement he'd just delivered as if it were of no consequence. "How? When—"

"I am a private investigator."

His words seemed to echo in the air.

And just that easily, it made sense to Kate. She had no doubt that Brett would deny it, but she also had no doubt that his unswerving career choice—known to him even when he was barely a teenager—was tied up with issues of his father. No matter how often she'd asked him in the past how he *knew* so surely how he wanted to spend his life, he'd never said.

But now—all these years later—she understood. "Where is he?"

"Dead."

A fresh wave of shock hit her. "Oh, Brett. I'm sor—"

"Don't be. He was a drunk. And he died, a felon, in prison, Kate. Which pretty much proved the opinion your father had of me."

"Daddy didn't—"

"You know as well as I do that Caine didn't think I was fit to breathe the same air as a Stockwell. If he knew that I was working on the case to find Madelyn, he'd probably find some stubborn way to cheat Death out of his due just to get rid of me."

"He does know. I, um, I told him." Kate swallowed. She rose restlessly and deposited her wrapper and napkin into the trash bin. "The morning we left for Boston.

Except that I'm not sure he even understood who I was.''

"Why tell him, then?"

"I needed to, Brett. Daddy pretty well ignored me my entire life. I needed to let him know that I was doing something active. And to, well, to say goodbye.'' Pain settled in her stomach, with all the relentless familiarity of an unwelcome relative.

She looked across the park.

A young woman was pushing a stroller toward the collection of playground equipment, complete with a square sandbox. A trio of teenagers were tossing around a Frisbee. On a bench on the opposite side of the park, an elderly man and woman sat together. She, reading a book. He, tossing crumbs at the pigeons clustered around the brick path.

They looked like a perfectly matched pair. Content with a lifetime of happiness behind and before them.

"I had no idea how long we'd be here in Boston," she said quietly. "And, whether I want to face it or not, Daddy's condition is worsening by the day. He could live three hours or three days or three months at this point. I didn't want to leave without…without saying it.'' She looked over at him. "Just in case. Is that so awful?''

His eyes were dark and filled with something she couldn't name. "No. Not awful. Nobody likes to end things unfinished.''

Suddenly Kate wasn't sure just exactly who they were talking about anymore. "Right," she said faintly. "Everyone deserves a goodbye.''

"Yes," he agreed steadily. "Everyone does.''

And they both knew that, eight years ago, between the two of them, it was the one word that neither one had said.

Chapter Ten

A hard, flat disc of bright orange plastic sailed between them, landing at Brett's feet.

The thick, suffocating tension that had arisen between them was just as unexpectedly broken.

Brett leaned over and picked up the Frisbee, sending it flying back to the kids with an easy expertise. And Kate realized that not all memories were painful.

She and Brett and Hamilton and whoever else was there at the time, chasing around on hot summer days. Either on Stockwell grounds, or at the Orwell estate. It hadn't mattered where they were. Only that they were all together. That they were all friends.

Frisbees. Footballs. Baseballs. Horseback riding, fishing, swimming.

In just that moment, Kate remembered it all, and it washed over her in a soothing wave.

One of the teens caught the Frisbee with a wave and

a shouted "thanks." Brett threw away his empty water bottle and turned to her.

"We should get started again."

She nodded and followed him out of the relative peacefulness of the green park to the busier sidewalk. "You don't want to wait to hear from Mr. Maldovan?"

"There's no point in sitting on our thumbs doing nothing until we find out."

Kate couldn't argue. She knew that things were much safer between her and Brett when they could actively concentrate on their task. "Which gallery is next?"

He rattled off three, complete with street addresses and took her elbow as they crossed the busy corner. They walked for a few hilly blocks, then found the gallery in question. Brett opened the door for her and they stepped into the cool interior. He was already pulling the snapshot from his pocket.

Within minutes, they knew that this particular dealer wasn't the one they sought. Kate wandered around, looking at the paintings and sketches while Brett continued conversing with the art dealer, trying to draw out any information that might possibly turn out to be useful.

When he joined her, Kate was standing in front of a large, square canvas covered in dark, bold brushstrokes.

"Anybody who hangs that in their living room is asking for nightmares," he said after a moment.

"Not necessarily." She pointed at the small card hanging on the wall next to the painting. "It's entitled *Cleansed*."

"Yeah, well, it looks to me like the artist should have *cleansed* his paintbrush a little more often."

She smiled faintly. "It's a cathartic painting, Brett. Surely you can see that. Sense it."

"It looks like the inside of a serial killer's mind to me," he countered.

"See a lot of those, do you, to recognize it when you see it?" She rolled her eyes and looked from him back to the painting. It reminded her strongly of little Bobby Morales's childish work. "Creativity is a tangible means of getting your feelings out in the open. Where they're less overwhelming and more manageable. You look at this and see pain. I look at it and see the freeing of one's pain."

She felt his curious look, and flushed a little. "Not exactly a textbook description of what I do," she answered his unspoken question, "but close enough."

"Do your patients have a lot of cleansing to do?"

Kate sighed faintly, and surprised them both, she decided, when she answered honestly. "Yes. They do."

"Yet you came to Boston."

Her jaw tightened.

"Don't get all offended," he murmured. "I'm not judging. I was just curious how you managed the time away from your caseload, seeing as how you're often traveling around the state to see your patients."

She looked at him. "How did you know that?" She wasn't entirely sure how she felt about him being so familiar with her life.

"I'm a professional snoop, remember?" His voice was smooth as he guided her out onto the street.

More hilly blocks. Kate's legs were beginning to tire. She'd walked more in the past few days than she had in the past few months. The results, when they got there, were the same. Strikeout.

Even though they'd been dining on a steady diet of art galleries, Kate found herself lingering in this one while Brett, once again, did his usual probing.

It was large and airy and smelled of lavender. And instead of using walls or partitions to display the artwork, the paintings—all sans frames—were hung, suspended from the beamed ceiling above by invisible wires. It was different and eye pleasing.

"Now *that,* I like," Brett said when he joined her. "Naked woman. Very nice."

Kate shook her head. She knew good and well that Brett was being deliberately obtuse. "A Nude. A beautiful nude, certainly. But it is *art,* so stop drooling before you draw attention to yourself."

"Call it art if you want," he said, eyes amused. "To me, it's a naked woman."

"A naked woman carrying a five-figure price tag," Kate said dryly.

"I remember when you had that nekkid guy prancing around for that one class you took."

She couldn't help but laugh. "He wasn't prancing, and he wasn't *nekkid.* He was a professional artist's model and we were studying human form."

"He had that, all right."

Kate's gaze slid to Brett. For a subject, Brett would have been—and still would be—even more perfect a specimen than the model. But she didn't think his healthy ego needed to hear that. "Jealous?"

Brett snorted and drew her outside. "Of that pretty boy? Hardly. Who the hell goes into a classroom full of wet-behind-the-ears students and sprawls out in all his glory on a velvet couch?"

"Stop making it sound naughty," she sputtered, laughing despite herself. "It was a class assignment."

"Flirting?"

"I did not flirt with him!"

"Could have fooled me. I came to pick you up that

day when your car battery died and it was just the two
of you in the classroom. You and Mr. Bare wearing
nothing but a robe. Looked like flirting to me.''

"He was gay," Kate countered, remembering the in-
cident. "And he was telling me about his recent worst-
date-in-history experience."

"Gay or not, the guy was flirting with you, Katy."

And Brett had been supremely annoyed, as Kate re-
called. She'd believed it was because she'd needed him
to pick her up and he'd had to leave early from his job
where he worked with an investigator for a large legal
firm to do so.

"I wanted to plant my fist in his face," Brett said.
"But I didn't want to end his pretty-boy career. Figured
the guy probably had no other visible means of support."

Kate shook her head, still laughing. "You're terrible."

The corner of his lips deepened. "Yeah, but you love
me, anyway."

Her smile stayed in place, but it took an effort. It was
just a flip remark; the same kind he'd made—often—
when they were younger.

Fortunately they arrived at their next destination.

Unfortunately it was another strikeout.

This time, it was Kate who joined Brett where he
was looking at the painting situated in center place of
the display window.

"Looks like oatmeal," he said to her.

Kate couldn't disagree. "It's mixed media. Acrylics
and handmade paper."

"Still looks like oatmeal. I could cook some up and
fling it at my walls. Be a helluva lot cheaper than buying that thing."

She shook her head. "Prefer the naked lady, do you?"

His eyes were amused. "I'm a healthy, red-blooded American male, princess. What do you think?"

She thought that he was wholly dangerous when he was in this wry, amused mood. "I think you're a typical man. Thinking with his—"

"Hey, hey, hey. There are children around."

Kate snorted softly and followed him back out onto the street only to find herself herded by Brett along with a crowd of office workers heading toward the T. The subway barely stopped before they were all piling on, filling seats and every other space known to mankind.

Kate could either lean back against Brett, or she could be pressed up against a complete stranger.

She chose Brett.

He had one hand on the loop to steady them and the other around her. Circling her wrist. Thumb moving—absently?—against the flesh on the inside.

She closed her eyes for a moment, undone by that small motion.

Then realized that his thumb had paused. "Scars," he muttered above her ear.

She blinked, calling for coherency. "Excuse me?"

His expression was unreadable as he looked down at her. "Your scars. From the bones you broke. One of them went through the skin."

Her mouth went dry. The accident. He was talking about the accident. "Yes." She had to push out the word past lips gone numb.

"And you gave up your dreams of becoming a famous artist."

She frowned a little. She couldn't tell if he was being serious or being facetious. That dream of being a "famous artist'' had been about as formed and well thought out as her dream of being an airline pilot. It wasn't until after she'd graduated with a degree in fine arts and no clue what she'd wanted to do with it, that she'd finally begun to search for something that had some meaning in it.

No, her conscience countered. *It was only after Brett abandoned you that you began searching.* Until then, she'd believed that marrying him and beginning a family was all that she'd needed to make her feel as if she had a real place in the world.

Only Brett hadn't wanted to set a date and she'd been left, watching him move further and further away from her as he pursued his career. They'd been engaged for two years, an engagement that *she* had asked for, yet. She'd been losing him and she'd known it.

She was saved from responding to his comment, however, by the sudden lurch of the subway as it stopped. Unloaded. Then loaded, growing ever more crowded. Then it lurched again and his hand kept her from lurching with it. She glanced up at him, automatic thanks on her lips.

And realized just how tired he really looked.

Distress curled through her. She knew she'd been wrapped up in her own emotional upheaval, but to have it advertised so obviously to her now, shamed her. She spent her life helping others, yet with Brett that normal behavior seemed to simply short-circuit.

Her teeth sank into her lip as she continued looking at him. It wasn't as if he looked ready to drop. Far from it. And unless a person knew him well, they wouldn't see his weariness in the line that scored his cheek. In the angle of his lips or the brooding heaviness of his lids.

Then Kate looked forward, startled at her own thoughts. She didn't know Brett well. Not anymore.

She wasn't sure she'd ever known him, when it came down to it. Because the man she'd thought she'd loved, the man she'd planned to spend her life with, wouldn't have been the man who walked away from her without a "goodbye."

Yet that is exactly what he'd done.

Sighing, Kate stared at the back of the man standing in front of her. She hoped that Mr. Maldovan was their "guy" as Brett had put it.

Because as torn as she was over finding Madelyn, she was even more torn by Brett's nearness and the fact that, no matter how painful the past was, nothing could have been changed. And the future loomed before her, just as empty.

Brett looked at the dim glow of his watch. Two in the morning.

He leaned back in the side chair and propped his legs on the bed opposite him. But his back twinged badly and he finally stood. As he did so, his elbow knocked against Kate's heavy sketch pad and it slid off the table, hitting the floor, loose pages scattering.

He stared at them. In all the years he'd known Kate, she'd never once offered him a glimpse at her sketch pad. And now, there were at least a half-dozen pages scattered on the carpet. She'd have a fit if she knew he'd seen any of them. He couldn't blame her. There were things in his briefcase that he'd sure in hell not want *her* to see—the engagement ring he'd once given her being at the top of that particular list.

But the drawings were just laying there. The top one stared up at him. A beautiful, yet spare, sketch of a woman…an older version of Katy…separated by an eon of space from a younger woman. Kate herself.

It was a testament to Kate's incredible artistic ability. And it made something deep inside him ache. Every single line of the sketch screamed loneliness. And he'd never made any pretenses of being particularly sensitive to visual art.

He leaned over and carefully straightened the pages, getting glimpses of babies, a young boy with soulful eyes. There were a few flowers, vivid and exotic looking. And a sketch of him that made him wonder if he really did look that grim all the time.

He pushed them all back into the portfolio and set it back on the table. His thumb moved over the edge of the sturdy, leather cover. He knew without a doubt that it was the same cover that she'd used eight, ten, twelve years ago. Jack had given it to her for her high school graduation present. Custom-made to hold the oversize spiral-bound art pads she favored inside. Her name had been engraved on it, but the gold lettering had obviously long since faded.

How many times when they'd been together had she retreated with her pad when she'd been troubled, or tense, or just flat-out annoyed?

She was still doing it to this day. Sketching out her heart. Her feelings. Her secrets into which—no matter how unintentionally—he'd gotten a glimpse.

She'd graduated from college with a degree in fine arts. Yet, two years later, while she'd still been married to Ham, Brett knew that she'd gone back to study psychology.

He exhaled roughly and pushed the sketch pad back onto the table, toward the middle where it couldn't be knocked around again. Then he moved to the glass door, deliberately forgetting about the images he'd seen inside that leather sketch pad cover.

Outside the window, the night was silvered by the moon. He blew out another long breath, thinking about the day.

About Kate's excitement when they'd gotten the lead about Maldovan. Her pretty blue eyes had lit like there was some magical pixie dust glistening inside. And her smile. God, her smile was enough to make a grown man weak.

She'd even harped on him about getting more rest all through dinner. Dinner, which consisted of piping-hot, thick-crusted, gooey, spicy pizza and a freeze-your-tongue-off cold beer that he'd passed up in favor of a soda. Dinner that she ate as if she'd never eaten before in her life.

She'd ordered it all and he'd been struck dumb when the food arrived, not under silver domes on top of white linen. But in unpretentious, greasy cardboard and a brown paper sack.

They'd eaten, sitting barefoot on the bed, with the pizza between them and a deck of cards that she'd pulled from her suitcase. They'd played gin.

She'd trounced him.

And he'd wanted her.

He exhaled roughly, raking his hair back with one hand and looking again at the bed. He'd been on-line with his office for hours; both during and after Kate's bath. He at least had the satisfaction of knowing that little Amy had been finally retrieved from her father's clutches, even though Brett hadn't been able to be there when it all went down.

It was the result that counted. Not his sense of having left one case for another.

He'd had to shift priorities with cases before in a kind of triage with incoming cases. His firm had so many that his personnel manager was already looking for more support staff. Another PI.

God. He was doing everything but stand on his head to put off going to bed. It hadn't seemed so bad when, on the other nights, he'd joined her to soothe her from her nightmares. But tonight, she was sleeping as sound as sound could be.

He rubbed his palm down his face and finished flicking open the buttons on his shirt. He tossed it on the chair and automatically reached for his fly.

Then thought better of it.

In her sleep, she'd taken her half of the bed right smack out of the middle. He sat down on the very edge of the mattress, nearly laughing at his own caution. Only Kate had ever driven him to such extremes. And he liked it as little now as he had back when he was twenty-two and trying like hell to make something of his life so their future together would be more than just food stamps and wishful dreams and the dinky, cramped apartment that they'd kept secret from her family and from his mother, before she'd died during their sophomore year.

And then Kate's hand touched his, nearly jolting him right out of his skin as he was yanked to the present and the reality of Kate Stockwell, sleepy and warm and desirable.

"Lay down with me, Brett," she murmured sleepily. "Get some sleep."

He looked down at her. Saw the liquid gleam of her eyes in the moonlit night. Then she withdrew her hand, tucked it beneath her cheek with the other and went silent again.

Asleep.

There wasn't a muscle in his body that wasn't crying for more than the measly few hours of sleep he'd allowed it on the other nights. Since that first night, he'd made damn sure to be awake and out of bed well before she awoke. If she even knew he'd slept in that bed beside her since that first night, for even the barest of minutes, he couldn't be sure. They sure hadn't discussed it.

Feeling like a damn fool, Brett forced himself to stretch out beside her on that mattress that should have been wider, but wasn't.

Mr. Control.

What a bloody joke.

He turned his head, finding the pillow. Closed his eyes despite the busyness still going on inside his head, determined to keep him wakeful despite everything.

Then, beside him, Katy shifted and her half out of the middle suddenly became her half on his side. Despite the covers that cocooned her, her arm slid over his waist, hand sliding over his chest, finally stopping directly over his heart.

The fresh scent of her filled his head just as slyly as his arms were suddenly filled with the fresh reality of her.

He blew out a long breath, turned and tucked her, blankets and all against him. No nightmare tonight, he thought, yet she'd still turned to him in her sleep.

Then he closed his eyes, finally.

And slept.

Mrs. Hightower had forgotten to draw the drapes in Kate's bedroom. As a result, the morning light was shining across her bed, intruding on her sleep.

Kate drew in a long breath, shifted and turned, thinking to pull the pillow over her head and sleep a few minutes more. She had time. Her first appointments of the day were never before 10:00 a.m.

But as she shifted, she became aware of the warm, heavy weight of an arm across her waist.

Reality crashed down on her.

She wasn't home in her wide, lonely bed at the mansion.

She was in Boston, and as it had been that first non-morning-after, the wide hotel bed was filled with six-foot-three inches of slumbering male.

A male who grumbled a wordless protest as she moved. Who, with one smooth sweep, pulled her right back over to him, nearly on top of his hard, bare chest.

Kate couldn't help it. Her hand brushed across that broad plane before she realized it.

Shuddering, she dropped her head to his shoulder. She lay there, in his arms, until she could finally control the nerves that trembled through her. She looked up at his face. Jaw shadowed and blurred. Thick black-brown hair tousled, one lock falling over his angular face.

His mouth, softened in sleep, looking surprisingly full. Unexpectedly vulnerable.

And his thick, enviable eyelashes.

Aware of the danger of her perusal, she tried to slide out from the arms he'd crossed around her. But every time she tried, they merely tightened.

He'd always held her tightly when he slept. Right from the very first.

Maybe it was the early hour. Maybe it was the reality of waking up in his arms. But Kate couldn't keep the memories from flooding her mind. From coursing through her bloodstream like the sweetest wine.

* * *

"Are you sure?"

Kate trembled. Loving him so desperately. Wanting him more than she'd ever believed possible. Her hands slid over Brett's shoulders. "Yes," she whispered, shakily.

"This isn't romantic," he muttered. His black-brown hair was wild, disheveled from the swim they'd just taken in Stockwell Pond. "The hotel room we'd arranged—"

"Shhh." Kate shivered, but not from cold. They were soaking wet, wearing only their swimsuits, but the summer air was hot and heavy. What made her shiver was knowing that now, at long last, she and Brett were going to make love. Finally. She'd be his in every way.

And he would be hers.

"I'm sorry we fought the night of the prom," she told him. "I don't know what got into me. I was nervous—"

"So was I."

Kate sucked in her lip, staring up at Brett. He'd always seemed so assured. He always knew where he was going, he always had a plan, a goal. And she…well, her plans, her goals, changed fifty times a day, at least. The only thing consistent was her love for Brett. Right from the first. He'd been the only one for her.

He always would be.

"Are you nervous now?"

His hand cupped her jaw, thumb brushing over her lips. His warm brown gaze mesmerized her. "No. I don't want to hurt you, Katy. Not ever."

Heat swept through her cheeks. "You'd never hurt me, Brett."

"No?"

She smiled shakily. "No." Then she swallowed, des-

*peration making her brave as she reached behind her
and in a quick movement tugged loose the knot of her
bikini top. It fell away and Brett's eyes heated even
more. He'd seen her without her top before. But always
knowing that they were not going any further.*

*She swallowed again, moving up against him, stretch-
ing up to wrap her arms around his neck, her breasts
reveling in the sensation of his sprinkling of chest hair
against her body. She was trembling wildly and his
arms came around her, holding her close and secure.*

*"This is romantic enough for me, Brett," she whis-
pered against his neck. "This is where we came for
picnics when we were fifteen. Remember?" This was a
patch of tree-shaded grass on the very furthest reaches
of the pond. Where even the gardeners never managed
to go. It was wild and overgrown and it was their spot.
And theirs alone.*

*His large palms swept over her bare back, a fine
tremor in them. Then he was picking her up in his
strong, fine arms and carrying her to the softest mound
of grass where he laid her down and slowly reached
for the ties holding the two triangles of her bikini together high over her hips.*

*Kate shook. And Brett's gaze found hers. She put her
fingers over his, and pulled on the tie. His face was
tight, his eyes fierce as he finished the job, laying her
bare. He breathed in sharply, and Kate felt tears burning behind her eyes as she pulled him down to her,
pushing blindly at his own swimsuit.*

*And then it was just the two of them. Young and in
love and shaking. His eyes were wet, too, when Kate
couldn't help that first muffled gasp of pain. And then
his mouth was on hers and what they didn't yet possess*

in finesse, they more than made up for in youthful, innocent passion. It was the stuff dreams were made of.

It was beautiful and it was addicting.

It was love.

And after, when Brett lay in her arms, his head against her breasts, while the tears of joy slowly dried on her cheeks and their hearts slowly quieted, when they'd whispered of the future they'd have together, of the children they'd create together, Kate had been certain that every beautiful wish would come true.

How wrong she had been, Kate thought now. She'd stopped trying to escape Brett's hold, and almost immediately, magically, his hold eased.

Kate sucked in a hard breath, sternly reminding herself that she *wanted* to get free, and scooted away. Leaving the bed and the bittersweet memories behind.

He sighed in his sleep and in a motion that brought back so many other mornings that they'd awakened together, caught her pillow in his long-fingered grip and turned his face into it.

Kate fled, shutting herself in the bathroom. She blindly turned on the shower, threw off her pajamas and jumped beneath the water.

And then, only then, did she let the tears flow.

For all the things that hadn't been.

And for all the things that would never be.

Chapter Eleven

"No. I'm sorry. I did have a LeClaire pass through here, oh, about ten months ago, a fluke really. I handled the painting only because I'd already dealt with a few of her sculptures from the same owner. The painting went to a collector in France." Rolando Maldovan, fussy in bizarrely ruffled suit and neon boots, closed his eyes in thought. "Name of—"

"Roubilliard," Brett inserted.

Maldovan nodded. "Yes, that was it exactly. How did you know?"

Brett just shook his head. He knew, because it was the dealer that Jack had dealt with near Paris. Circles. They were going in circles. And though it was just one more part of the game that he'd chosen as his life's work, this time it annoyed him no end.

Mainly because he could tell by the still, pinched look on Katy's face that the news was killing her. She looked like a peachy, melony vision today in her sleeveless top and matching slouchy pants. The past few days tramping all over Boston had brought even more of a gilded tan to her skin and, were it not for the distress on her face that she was trying mightily to hide, she'd look just like an adored newlywed should look.

Maldovan had already made it clear that he didn't represent Madelyn. And the flamboyant man might not see Kate's distress, but Brett sure in hell did.

He'd been concerned about just this thing. Particularly when she'd come out of her shower that morning—a good four hours ago now—and he'd seen the vestiges of tears in her eyes.

"Do you remember what piece it was?" He asked the owner. It didn't matter in the overall scheme of things, but Brett had a habit of getting more details than he usually needed. And keeping the dealer talking would give Kate time to gather her shattered nerves.

Even now, she was turning away, walking toward an ugly green sculpture sprouting up out of a pot shaped like a foot. Brett pulled his gaze from the thing. Talk about beauty being in the eye of the beholder.

"Yes. I remember it quite well, actually," Maldovan was saying. "A small seascape. Right here on the Cape. Quite a lovely little piece, actually, despite the fact that it's not my usual cup of tea."

Brett nodded. More useless information. But that wasn't Maldovan's fault. "We appreciate your time."

"I'm sorry I wasn't more help. LeClaire's are gaining quite a reputation as investment pieces. Her sculptures haven't done too badly, either, though she's only done a few really modern pieces."

Brett nodded again. He wrapped his hand around Katy's cold one and headed toward the entrance.

"Actually, now that I think about it, you might check the Deane gallery, if you're looking for an oil," the fussy man called out as they pushed open the door.

Brett went still. He looked back at Maldovan. "Deane? Marissa Deane?"

The other man nodded. "She handles a number of artists of LeClaire's caliber. Much more traditional art, you know." His expression was vaguely bored.

"Her gallery has been closed for repairs," Brett prompted.

"Yes. Vandalism, I believe."

"The sign she posted indicated she'll be reopening tomorrow."

"Does it?" Maldovan lifted his shoulder, smoothed the strange ruffle, that was apparently supposed to be a tie, with a manicured hand. "I haven't spoken with her personally in some time. We don't run in the same circles. But she's probably your best bet if you're really set on procuring a LeClaire oil. I'm surprised, actually, that someone hasn't told you that, already."

Beside him, some of the color had returned to Kate's face. He could feel her hand suddenly tremble where he held it inside his. He thanked the gallery owner and guided Kate out the door.

Her eyes were wide and distressed and excited all at once. She looked like a kid who had been presented with her most wished-for gift; awed, moved and afraid to touch it for fear it would disappear.

He nudged her closer to the brick wall of the gallery. "You okay?"

Her throat worked on a swallow, then she nodded. And he watched as vulnerable Katy slowly disappeared beneath the calm facade of Kate Stockwell. "I'm fine," she said firmly.

But her lips trembled a little and he knew that the facade couldn't completely obscure the real woman inside.

He let out a breath, coming to a decision that he would no doubt regret later. "Okay, Kate. Here's the deal. We can spend the rest of the day tromping more galleries. Or I can see if I can locate this Marissa Deane woman before tomorrow morning."

Kate's eyes widened. "You can do that?"

He'd do just about anything to get the shaky, frightened look out of her eyes. Kate Stockwell in her bossy, humorous mode was hard enough to resist. Kate as a trembling, vulnerable woman, was making mincemeat of him. *This* was the woman who cried out in her sleep with nightmares that she wouldn't acknowledge during her waking hours.

"I can try," he corrected.

The pearly edge of her teeth worried her lip. "We'd probably look rather anxious. If you did find her, I mean."

"Possibly." No matter what he'd told her, Brett was still aware that if they tipped their hand too soon, Madelyn could easily bolt. There was just no way of knowing for sure. Not until they tracked her down and dealt with it. Face-to-face. Not until they learned her side of the story of her flight from Grandview twenty-nine years ago. "But we'll deal with that. So, what do you want to do?"

"Find Marissa Deane," Kate whispered.

Brett nodded. "All right then. Let's do it."

They went by the gallery first. The sign that had been there earlier that week was still in position and the building itself was locked up tighter than a drum.

Brett hailed a cab and they went back to the hotel,

and while Kate hovered anxiously beside him, he made some calls. A short while later, they were in another cab. No amount of work on his part had produced Deane's telephone number, but at least he'd obtained a home address.

"We should have done this earlier in the week," Kate murmured as the cab threaded its way through the congested traffic. "But then we didn't know that *she* was the one who might represent Madelyn."

Brett almost reached over to cover the hands that were clenched in a knot on her lap. "You always call her that," he said instead. "Madelyn."

"What should I call her?" Kate's voice was sharp. "Mother? We don't know for sure that she's our *mother.*" She turned her head, staring out the window beside her.

Since Brett was fairly certain that Madelyn *was,* he kept his mouth shut.

"A *mother* stays with her children," she said flatly.

Brett frowned. "Kate, you of all people should know that sometimes families can't stay together."

She looked back at him. "Why, *me* of all people?"

"Because of the work you do with your kids."

She seemed to pale. "My *patients,*" she corrected.

"All right. Your patients. You must see kids in your practice who are part of families that are better off apart than they were together."

"Bobby."

"Who?"

She shook her head, looking as if she regretted the admission. "Never mind."

"What?"

But again, she just shook her head, turning her attention out the side window.

Annoyance rose in him, swift and hard. "Dammit, Kate. Do you *ever* just say what's on your mind? Just put it out there, on the table?" Her hair flew as her head swiveled around to look at him as if he'd lost his mind. Perhaps he had. "Who's Bobby?" he asked again.

"None of your business."

"You brought him up, princess. Who is he?"

"He's a little boy who has the kind of family nobody should be saddled with," she said flatly. "And he's the reason I had the time to foist my company on you for this little New England jaunt. All right?"

No, it wasn't all right. "What's wrong with his family?"

"He is—was—a patient, Brett. You don't share your cases with me, I don't reveal confidential information with you."

"I told you about Amy."

Her face paled and his anger drained away, leaving him feeling a lot of things he didn't want to claim. The only thing he couldn't figure is why hearing the child's name affected her so. Hell, he remembered the day that they'd talked about names for the kids they'd one day have, but she was the one who'd married someone else. Why should it bother her now, to hear the name?

"I usually only take on one or two cases at a time, because the amount of time I spend with the children can be...considerable."

"So Bobby was your only case."

She nodded. "His mother died last year and his father is a recovering alcoholic who bows to pressure from his uptight parents who don't believe that therapy has any true benefit because of some religious thing they've got going. I don't begrudge them their beliefs, but Bobby's father isn't involved in that church, supposedly. He just doesn't have one solid piece of spine in him. I've devoted two months of working exclusively with Bobby and he's come so far, but now—'' she looked away ''—now I'm afraid he'll go back into his shell and never come out again.''

"Lots of kids have parents who die." It sounded callous, but it was true.

"Most kids aren't witness to their mother's murder."

He jerked, staring at her, truly surprised. Surprised? Hell, she'd shocked the daylights out of him. "Murdered?"

"Yes. Nobody believes Bobby, though. His grandparents insist that Bobby's mother committed suicide."

"And the dad?"

"The dad started with good intentions, I think. His son was not getting through his grief, and in what I'd consider a rare bit of good sense on his part and good luck for Bobby, he sought help through a colleague of mine. Bobby wouldn't even speak at first, which is how I came to be involved."

"He drew pictures?"

"Essentially."

"What do the police say?"

"Nothing. I've tried several times to get them to look more closely, but their answer is always the same. There was no reason to disbelieve the suicide theory."

"But you don't believe it."

"I've worked with Bobby," she said simply.

He didn't know what to say. Being speechless wasn't something he was closely familiar with. Then he realized the cab had pulled to a stop in front of an elegant brownstone. "We're here."

Kate's expression, the one that had grown fierce as a lioness as she'd discussed Bobby, shifted and paled again. He asked the cabby to wait and then he tucked his hand under Kate's elbow as they headed up the stone walk. Through that small touch, he could easily detect Kate's tension.

"Remember, this may not pan out."

"I remember. But it could just as easily *work* out, couldn't it?"

He nodded and pushed his finger against the buzzer beside the door. But after a long, fraught moment, it was obvious that the buzz wouldn't be answered. He tilted his head back, looking up at the tall, narrow building. Kate headed down the steps and walked around the side of the house. He buzzed several more times and peered through the big picture window on the front of the building, to no avail.

Then Kate returned. "She's not here," she told him huskily. "The man who lives behind this one said she's been in Europe. He watches her cat, apparently."

He wasn't going to question how Kate had elicited the information from a complete stranger. "Did he happen to say when she is expected to return?"

"Tomorrow morning."

"Just in time for her gallery to reopen."

"Apparently."

He blew out an impatient breath. "Well, then we wait until tomorrow."

"We can visit the rest of the galleries on the list."

They could. Except Brett could see the disappointment clouding her eyes, rounding her shoulders. She needed a break. He needed a break.

He tucked his hand around her arm. "Come on." He tugged her back to the cab. "We're not going to the next gallery," he said abruptly.

She eyed him. "Then...where are we going?"

"To breakfast. Or brunch, if you prefer. Doesn't matter, as long as it's food, princess. I'm hollow inside, and that half apple you nibbled on earlier when we left the hotel can't be sustaining you too well, either." He didn't wait for the argument from her that was sure to follow. "Then we're going to take the rest of the afternoon off and play tourist."

Her lashes lowered, hiding whatever was in her eyes from him. "Really?"

"Really. I can break out my cuffs if need be, Kate. But it'd be a helluva lot easier if you'd just go along without arguing."

At that, her lashes lifted. And he couldn't read her expression to save his soul. "First off, I don't think you even own a pair of handcuffs. And secondly, have I protested?"

"You will. It's just a matter of time."

The cab turned a corner at a fast clip and she leaned toward him, steadying herself with her hand on the door handle. "Then I'll just get it out of the way, shall I?"

"We're taking the afternoon off, Kate. That's all I have to say about it."

One smooth eyebrow lifted. "How are you going to explain *that* on your itemized accounting to your client?"

His sharp eyes filled with sardonic humor. "Personal time, princess. Even us foam cups are entitled to it."

"Foam cup?"

"You know. Foam. Ordinary. Inexpensive. Opposite end of the spectrum from you china types."

"I didn't know you were into labels so much," she said. "And aside from the fact that foam cups are probably as widely used, if not more so, than china...we both know that you're miles from ordinary. You've got the man-in-charge persona firmly in place, Brett. And it's been there since we were kids.''

He made a disbelieving sound. "I washed and waxed Judge Orwell's fleet of cars for lunch money," he reminded flatly.

"So? You were, what? Fifteen or so? You had a job and you did it well. Where's the shame in that? You know, Brett, nobody thought less of you because you weren't born with the proverbial silver spoon. Nobody, except you."

His expression was unreadable. "And Caine."

"You didn't give two hoots for what my father thought of you and you know it."

"*You* cared what he thought."

She frowned, suddenly feeling out of her depth. It was a lamentably frequent occurrence when it came to him. "He is my father," she finally said. It covered it all. And covered nothing.

Fortunately the cab had stopped again. Brett paid the fare and climbed out, his hand extending back to her in a move so automatic that Kate felt sure he wasn't even aware of it.

Any more than he'd probably been aware of her that morning as anything other than a warm female body.

She put her hand in his and stepped from the vehicle, joining him on the sidewalk. A line of people snaked out the doorway of the narrow building in front of them. She looked from the line to Brett. "If that's where you're planning to eat, it'll be suppertime before we make it through that line."

He shook his head and an unexpected grin hovered around his lips. "It'll be fine. Trust me."

Just another one of those flip comments. Easily said. "Trust me." But Kate knew that she did trust Brett.

She trusted him to help her and her brothers find Madelyn and their unknown sibling.

She also trusted him to break her heart. All over again.

She knew they couldn't go back and recapture the past. She wasn't sure she even wanted to. Not when the man that Brett had become was so much...more than the boy that he'd been.

And she, well, she was so much less.

So there was simply no point in thinking along such lines at all.

Brett was tugging her through the crowded doorway, his tall, broad-shouldered body cutting a swath for Kate to follow. She caught at least a dozen annoyed looks thrown at them from the patrons waiting in line.

Then she heard a loud, deep voice call out his name and Brett was pulling her up to his side, as they burst through the tight confines of the entry into a mile-high building that rattled with the sound of dishes and conversation and laughter.

She stared when a man, the size of a mountain, descended on them, his striking ebony face wreathed in a beaming smile. "Brett, my man!" The mountain wrapped his arms around Brett in a hearty hug, and Kate knew her jaw just simply dropped when the other man practically lifted Brett right off his feet with the enthusiastic greeting.

She couldn't help but smile as Brett slapped the other guy on the back, a look of real pleasure on his face. Then the stranger turned to Kate and he stuck out a hand the size of a side of beef. Yet when she reached out to shake it, his touch was as gentle as a lamb.

"Kate Stockwell," Brett introduced, "this ugly mug

is an old friend of mine. Tommy Morton. Owner and operator of this dive.''

''Kate.'' Tommy looked at her closely, then glanced back at Brett and she instinctively knew that Tommy had heard her name before.

Probably not under glowing circumstances, she figured. Before she and Brett had split up, they'd pretty well known every one of each other's friends. There was no way she could have forgotten this man whose sheer size dwarfed even Brett's own healthy six-three.

''Got a table for us somewhere, Tommy?'' Brett asked.

''For you, man, anything.'' Tommy turned and looked around, calling out the name of a frazzled looking waitress before she could clear one of her tables in preparation of seating someone else. ''Save that table for my pal Brett and his lovely lady.''

Kate's lips parted, an automatic demurral at the ready. But neither Brett nor Tommy were paying her any heed as they headed toward the table in question.

She shrugged mentally and followed them.

The aromas coming from the open kitchen were tantalizing and delicious and her stomach told her that she *was* hungry. She might feel like each knot inside her was first tightened, then joined by another, with every step that took them nearer to finding Madelyn LeClaire, but that didn't seem to be affecting her appetite at this particular moment in time.

The waitress finished cleaning the table just as they arrived at the table, and Brett waited for Kate to slide into the curving booth first. She scooted around to the back, then felt the space seem to shrink when the men joined her on either side.

Tommy handed her a menu with a gentle smile and

turned his attention back to Brett. "So what you doing in this neck of the woods, bud? Thought you gave up Boston 'bout the same time you gave up booze."

Kate blinked. Looked at Brett who was seriously ignoring her suddenly.

Then Tommy glanced at her and his eyebrows lifted. "Guess I put my foot in it again."

Brett shook his head, shrugging. "It's no secret," he said dismissively.

Only it was a big secret to Kate. Brett had never been much of a drinker. He'd always been too much in control. Yet this man, and Brett's response, seemed to say that, not only had he touched it, he'd touched it and given it up.

She watched him. How much more about this man was she unaware of?

"How's your wife?" he was asking Tommy.

Tommy grinned. "Pregnant, dude. Expecting number three in two months. Fatherhood is great, Brett. You oughta give it a try before you're too damn old to appreciate it."

Brett grinned hugely and Kate's newly burgeoning appetite withered. She looked down at her menu, staring blindly at it as the two men caught up with each other's lives.

And Brett's purpose for being in Boston? "Just a case." He dismissed it oh-so-easily to his friend, Tommy.

Suddenly she felt ill.

Just a case. *Just* someone he once knew. *Just* an unwanted daughter. *Just* a useless shell of a woman.

"Kate?"

She looked up to find both men watching her. And knew she'd completely missed whatever they'd said. In her lap, her free hand curled, fingernails digging into her palm. "Sorry?"

"Whatcha want to order?" Tommy prompted. "Anything your heart desires whether it's on the menu or not. Nothing's too good for my friend Brett and his pretty lady in peach."

Kate started to breathe again. Tommy was simply too friendly to not respond to it. Nevertheless, she honestly wasn't sure she could even stomach food just now. "Wheat toast and a cappuccino, please."

She was aware of Brett's eyebrow lifting, but refrained from looking at him.

"You need some protein, Katy," he said. "Add eggs to that," he told Tommy. "Poached. No. On second thought, make it eggs Benedict instead."

"Will do, man." Tommy slid from the booth and headed away, yelling out their order in a deep voice that carried over all of the racket inside the boisterous restaurant.

"I don't *want* eggs Benedict," Kate said flatly.

"Why not? You love it. And Tommy's is some of the best."

"I don't love it anymore."

"Since when?" He was looking at her much too closely. "You're pale. What's wrong?"

She carefully squared the silver knife and fork with the edge of the table. "I don't eat eggs Benedict anymore, and I don't appreciate your high-handedness."

His eyes narrowed. "It's just eggs Benedict, princess."

"It's upgrading to first class," she countered, wishing she could just take back saying anything at all. Wishing that she was better at hiding her feelings, wishing that she didn't look at him and…and *yearn* for things that would never be.

Brett absorbed that. Realized it was, to some extent, true. He'd taken the decision out of her hands as surely as she'd done with him. Both of them, just deciding what was best for the other. One step forward, three steps back.

It didn't—shouldn't—matter in the least to him what she ate.

Except that he remembered the days when they'd been living in that dinky apartment, and Sunday mornings had been just for them. When he wasn't working and she wasn't painting. When he wasn't studying and she wasn't hustling back to Stockwell Mansion to put in an appearance.

Sunday mornings with Kate. Music on the radio, sunshine streaming across their bed with the sag in the middle that meant they were constantly rolling toward each other.

Hot coffee, newspaper sections strewn across the bed and eggs Benedict that she'd ordered in from a nearby restaurant. Having it delivered, hot and fragrant, right to the apartment they were secretly sharing, paying a damned fortune for the privilege. But he hadn't been able to argue the extravagance, because she'd loved it.

And he'd loved her.

"Then change the order back to what you want," he said, blocking off the memories that had flooded his brain way too easily. "Eat toast or don't eat toast. Pass out later today, because you haven't eaten enough to keep a bird alive and sooner or later it's bound to catch up with you."

Her lips parted, prepared to speak, but the waitress appeared with her cappuccino and Brett's orange juice.

Kate's slender fingers surrounded the oversize ceramic mug. She didn't look at him. Her dark hair slid forward, toward her cheeks. But not far enough to obscure the sight of the silvery tear slowly creeping down her cheek.

The anger inside him drained away, leaving him feeling…hell, he didn't know what he felt. He only knew that she was out of his reach, just as much now as she'd ever been in the past.

The walls around her were in place and about ten miles high. Only problem was they were clear glass walls, and he could see through them to her, knowing she was hurting and not being able to do one damned thing about it.

She didn't call the waitress over to change the order. He drank his orange juice with knuckles gone white. And they sat there, silent, while all around them, cheer seemed to hang in the air of the crowded restaurant. Their food was delivered, Tommy came by to see if it was okay, then headed off again as raised voices filled the open kitchen area with even more confusion.

"How long have you known Tommy?"

Kate's quiet question surprised him. He looked at her, but she was focused on her eggs Benedict. Tearing it apart with tense little jabs of her fork.

He wasn't giving any better justice to his omelet, though. And he had to give her credit for trying to maintain some normalcy in a situation that was anything but.

He set down his fork and reached for the mug of hot black coffee that Tommy had poured for him on one of his passes by. "Seven years."

She nodded a little, still staring down at her plate. "He seems like a…popular man. I don't think I've ever been in a restaurant quite this busy. Where'd you meet?"

"Right here in Boston. He used to be a cop."

Kate's eyebrows lifted a little. "Oh. So…what? You met through a case or something?"

"No," Brett said evenly, "we met when he broke up a bar fight."

Kate's blue gaze lifted finally from her plate. "Oh. I see."

But it was obvious to him that she didn't. "I was one of the fools fighting," he said flatly. And waited for the shock, the disgust, to roll over her expression.

But, he just kept on waiting. Because her expression didn't change, except for a faint widening of her eyes. "Why?"

His jaw ached from holding it so tightly. "Because I was drunk, Kate. And stoned out of my mind on pain-killers."

Her fork clattered to the plate. "Brett—"

He exhaled roughly. "Look, just forget it. Tommy's been a good friend."

"You never used to drink anything other than a beer now and then," she said after a thick moment. "You didn't even drink one with our pizza last night. And painki—"

"I don't drink when I'm on a case."

Kate looked at him, wanting so desperately to understand what was going on behind his unreadable brown eyes. But it felt as if an ocean of pain separated them, and as soon as she stepped foot in the water, she'd sink like a stone. "Right," she whispered. "You're on a case. Stupid of me to keep forgetting that." She dropped her napkin on the table and began scooting out the far side of the curving booth. Her throat was strangled tight, but she pushed out the hoarse words anyway. "Particularly since it is *our* case."

''Where are you going?''

She shook her head, needing escape. Escape from the past that had gone so wrong. Escape from the future that would never hold the things she'd spent a lifetime dreaming of. But mostly from the present and this man who made her feel things she was better off not feeling. ''I just have to…go. I have to—''

He stepped out of the booth, moving faster than a man his size should be able to move, and caught her shoulders in his hands. ''You're not walking out on me, Katy. Not this time.''

She twisted, her vision glazed with tears. But he didn't let her loose. ''Brett—''

''Everything okay here?''

Kate's head jerked around and she stared, dismayed, at Tommy, who was standing behind them with a faint frown on his face.

''Yeah,'' Brett said before she could form a single word. ''You got someplace—a back—''

''Through the kitchen,'' Tommy said. ''Up the stairs.''

Brett's hands slid from her shoulders down to her wrist. ''I want to get *away* from you,'' she choked, twisting against his implacable hold, ''not go somewhere *with* you.''

He didn't respond. Just led her, inexorably, through the open kitchen, pushing through the swinging door in the rear, and tugging her up the narrow flight of stairs. It was either keep up with him or create an awful scene.

At the top of the stairs was a louvered door and Brett shoved it open, stopping it from bouncing back on them with the flat of his hand as he drew her inside.

Then the door was shut. Closing them inside a narrow office crammed with filing cabinets, a desk and chair and a well-used-looking couch. It was as if they'd hit another planet far away from the noisy chaos downstairs.

And now all she could hear was the sound of her pulse beating inside her head and Brett's steady breathing as he let go of her wrist and leaned back against the door, blocking the exit.

Kate rubbed her wrist with her other hand. He hadn't hurt her with his grip, but her skin burned like an aftershock from his touch. She couldn't bear to look at him, standing there, arms crossed, expression dark as he watched her.

"I didn't hurt your wrist," he said flatly.

She swallowed, dropping her hands, pushing them into the side pockets of her loose-fitted slacks. She turned away and stared blindly out the tall, narrow window. "No," she admitted rawly. "You didn't hurt my wrist."

"Not this time, anyway."

Kate's stomach seemed to drop away. Always the accident. Everything kept turning back to the accident. To that point in time when everything that had mattered to her had been irrevocably lost. Everything…Brett.

She slowly turned back around to look at him. To face him. "Not any other time, either," she said huskily.

His lips twisted. "How many bones were broken, Katy? In how many places?"

She slowly held out her right arm, inner wrist—scars white and nearly invisible—displayed. She wriggled her fingers, agile and strong. "All healed, Brett." It had taken two complicated surgeries and a year of therapy, but it had healed. "And it wasn't your fault, any more than it was mine. The other driver was at fault, pure and simple.''

She swallowed, lowering her arm once more. ''I didn't lose my 'dream' career because of the accident, Brett. I didn't lose anything in the accident.''

His dark eyes ensnared her.

She drew in a slow breath.

''Except you,'' she finished.

Chapter Twelve

Except you.

Her words hung in the air.

Kate longed to pull them back in, to pretend she hadn't said them. To pretend that she was as cool and removed and impervious as everyone seemed to believe. But she couldn't.

And she couldn't even begin to read what Brett was thinking behind his utter stillness.

"You didn't lose me, Kate," he finally said. "You drop-kicked me away. And I don't know what the hell kind of game this has become for you."

Her jaw loosened. "Game? Trust me, Brett, I'm not having a grand time here." The words didn't come out good and tart the way she'd planned. And her eyes ached with the pressure of tears she refused to shed.

"Then what *are* you having, Katy?" Brett pushed away from the door, beyond patience. "You say you didn't blame me for the accident. If that were true, why the hell wouldn't you even let me see you in the hospital?''

She blanched and her eyebrows pulled together. ''What?''

''Oh, come on, Kate,'' Brett said impatiently. ''You know damn well I nearly tore the walls down trying to get to you. I could see you laying in the bed when I finally found out what room they'd secreted you to. You didn't say one word.''

Then he swore, sharp and pungent, when she swayed. He pushed her unresistingly down onto the couch. She sat there, hunched, looking at him, her face about as riddled with pain as that damned painting—*Cleansed*—that they'd jokingly argued over.

Only this was no joke.

''You were at the hospital?''

He shoved his fingers into his jeans to keep from reaching for her. ''What do you mean? Of course I was. Where the hell else would I have been?''

She moistened her lips, staring down at her twisting, white-knuckled hands. ''I don't remember anything about the accident except our argument at the wedding reception right before we got in the car. And then, that truck…heading for us.''

''Argument.''

Her throat worked. ''When you told me that…if I wanted to get married so badly—''

''—you should find yourself another guy.'' He'd said it in anger, in a stupid, youthful fit of jealousy and pain and need for her to get just a hint of how much he was hurting, too. ''I believe what I said, Kate, was that if you wanted a fancy wedding right that minute so damned bad, to throw one with someone else.''

Not that it really made any difference at all. The results were what they were.

She didn't answer. Just looked toward the window. And he may well want to throttle her on a regular basis, but there was no denying the pain on her face.

Her teeth were holding her lower lip captive and her blue eyes shimmered with tears.

Well, dammit, he hurt, too. "And that is exactly what you did," he finished flatly. "Not even a year later, you were walking down the aisle with my pal Ham, in the splashiest society wedding Grandview had ever seen. Just the kind of wedding you'd been talking about since we were in high school."

She pressed her shaking fingertips to her forehead. "Can we just leave Hamilton out of this?"

"Oh, hell, yeah, Katy. We can leave him out of it." Brett snorted. "He was your *husband.* You stood in front of a minister and took vows with him. With someone *else.*"

Her gaze lifted to his. "I didn't know, Brett. I swear to you, I didn't know." Her lashes fell. She sniffed and swallowed, and he could see her struggling for composure.

"Didn't know *what?* That you were standing there in a church with someone who *was not me?* You were the one that brought up getting married in the first place, do you remember that?"

Her jaw went tight. "Being the one to propose to you isn't something I'm likely to forget." Then her eyes flickered. "I didn't know that you came to the hospital."

"Right."

"I didn't." She wrapped her arms at her waist, looking as if she was in physical pain.

Maybe she was. God knows his gut felt like he'd been kicked by a bull.

"When I was conscious again, I asked for you, Brett. You weren't even a patient at the hospital. Nobody would tell me anything. I thought…I thought at first that you were—" she closed her eyes, and a tear slid, achingly slow, down her cheek "—dead. And that they wouldn't tell me because I'd have wanted to die, too."

Her husky words seemed to echo around the confines of the small office. Leaving destruction wherever they hit.

Brett tilted his head back, looking somewhere for patience, for forgiveness, because he wished with every fiber of his soul just then that Caine Stockwell would roast in hell.

He roughly shoved a stack of menus off the metal footlocker in front of the couch and sat down directly in front of Kate. Yanked his folded handkerchief from his pocket and pushed it into her hand. Watched her trembling fingers curl slowly around it.

He raked his fingers through his hair and blew out a long breath. "I checked myself out," he said when he was sure he could speak without cursing her dying father right to her face. "The morning after."

Her throat worked. "Then you *were* hurt. Jack said—"

"What?" Brett felt murderous.

"He said you must have been hurt, but he couldn't find any information on you. Not in the police report, even, that only stated you'd been driving. Other than that…nothing."

Caine, Brett thought again. But at least it hadn't been Jack. Jack, whom he'd once considered a friend. Whom he still respected even if circumstances had long ago put an end to the other.

He rubbed his hand down his face. "If there was no information to be found, it's only because someone got rid of it."

"Jack talked to the emergency room doctors and nurses. He even checked the apartment, but you weren't there."

"You think I'm lying."

"No!"

He muttered an oath. "Your *father* stood in the doorway of your hospital room and told me that you refused to see me. That you wanted me to leave you alone. That the engagement was off."

She moistened her lips, obviously torn. "No. Daddy wouldn't have done that. He—"

"He what? Kate, come on. Open your eyes."

"But he knew I wanted to marry you," she murmured, nearly inaudible.

"And he wanted you to make a better match," Brett countered flatly. It all made a grim sort of sense. On the rare occasions that Brett had actually run across Caine at the mansion, the older man had made no secret of his opinion. "He wanted you to marry someone of your own class. Someone that would benefit your family. And Caine had never made any secret of pushing you and Hamilton together whenever he could. Hell, the judge did the same thing. Think about the times the three of us ended up together because of something the judge said to Ham."

"But you and Hamilton...you were friends."

"Yeah, well, we pretty well grew up together, didn't we? In his parents' fancy house where my mother was the cook. But we were friends who never made any secret of the fact that we were both after you.''

She kept shaking her head. Unwilling to believe. Unable to believe. ''No. No. It's just not possible. What possible advantage would there have been to pair me with him?''

''Hell, Kate. You're not *that* naive.''

''But Hamilton hadn't even passed his bar exam yet,'' Kate countered shakily. ''Why on earth…oh. His father. Judge Orwell.'' She looked up, her expression pained. ''Daddy wanted a judge in his pocket, didn't he? It was the one thing he didn't have. And a future son-in-law who specialized in mineral rights wouldn't hurt, either. Never mind that Stockwell International has an entire phalanx of legal eagles.''

There wasn't much more for Brett to add to that. And the silence between them lengthened. Thickened. And before his eyes, Kate seemed to just wilt. To fold in on herself. He had to wrap his fingers over the edge of the footlocker on either side of him to keep from reaching for her.

''It just keeps getting better and better, doesn't it?'' Kate finally said, her voice dull. ''My father. Caine Stockwell. Master manipulator. You believed him. I believed him. I was nothing to him—'' her lips trembled, firmed ''—but a pawn. A…useless…decorative… pawn.''

The hell with it. Brett wrapped his hands around hers. They were icy. There was still so much left unsaid. Unexplained. But for now, this moment right now, enough had been said. She couldn't take any more.

He wasn't sure he could, either.

He looked at her. Seeing the effort she was giving at

holding it together. At staying strong. At being Kate Stockwell.

Then he slid his hands up her forearms, to her shoulders and he simply hauled her limp form into his arms, onto his lap, holding her close. Burying his face in the warm satin of her fragrant hair.

She let out a gasping sob that reached down inside him and twisted the knots there even tighter. He pressed her head to his shoulder, felt her hands come around his waist. "It's okay, Katy."

Kate shook her head against him. "Nothing has been okay for years," she whispered.

Brett's shoulders moved. She felt his big, warm palm run over her hair. Down her back. "Ah, Katy." His voice was low, rasping over her. "Don't."

She swallowed, desperately scrambling for something, anything, to hold on to. To keep from losing control, because she wasn't sure if, once she did, she'd ever get it back again.

"Katy," he murmured against her ear. "It's okay, baby, just let it out. You don't have to hurt alone."

"I can't, Brett. I can't." She pulled her head away, looking at him. Seeing the sheen in his eyes, so dark, so melting.

And then he leaned the few inches forward between them and pressed his lips to her forehead.

Her shoulders shook.

"It's okay, baby." Another soft kiss to her eyes. Closing them. "I've got you."

But he didn't. Not really. And Kate knew that she wanted him to truly have her. In ways that she'd barely recognized when she'd been only twenty-two and had known she was losing him, inch by inch.

He'd known who he was and where he was going,

while she—she was a perennial bridesmaid who hadn't even known how to tell the man she'd loved for so very long that she was terrified of the widening gap between them. Him, moving closer and closer to his goals. She, falling behind, not knowing what to do with her life that was so suddenly changing from the relative haven and structure of their college days. She'd been losing him as surely as the sun rose each morning, and she'd been desperate to hold on to what they'd had.

Believing that if they could just get married, if she was just his wife—finally—that everything would have been all right.

And then, there in that cramped office, Brett's mouth covered hers.

And Kate was lost.

Tears leaked from her eyes and her lips opened against his, murmuring his name.

He lifted his head, his gaze meeting hers. He thumbed away a tear. "Katy. What the hell are we doing?"

"I don't know." She moistened her lips and let out a long, shaky sigh. "I don't care."

His fingers threaded through her hair, hands cradling her head. "You're still in my blood," he muttered.

"I'm sorry." She pushed her fingers through his hair. Shaping his beautiful head with her hands. Her face was wet with tears. "So sorry. So many things. Oh, Brett, I wish I—"

He exhaled. "Shhh." He pressed his mouth to hers again. Wide. Searching. Delving. Soothing.

His thumbs brushed away her tears, and then brushed away those that immediately replaced them. He kissed her and she wept for the bittersweet beauty of it. Of times past. Times lost. Times that would never come again, but right now, were so close, within touching distance, that she could nearly feel it under her fingertips.

His lips tasted of coffee and need. His name sang through her mind.

"Ah, Katy," he murmured roughly. Mouth burning over her jaw. Touching her neck just below her ear. Making her head arch back, suddenly breathless. Taunting her. Teasing her. Until she was twisting in his hold, pressing herself against him, mouth searching for his once more.

Needing him like her next breath. Shaking, wanting more, needing more—

And they both froze at the sound of footsteps pounding up the stairs outside the louvered door. She swallowed a protest when he moved, settling her back on the couch and rising, moving around the desk. Tension radiated from him while she felt as if she'd just been buffeted by a hurricane.

The door flew open and a young woman wearing the wait-staff uniform of khaki shorts and white shirt stood there, her expression clearly startled at finding them there. "Oh. Sorry." The girl smiled, but it was quick and awkward and Kate knew the inadvertent intruder was as uncomfortable at finding them as they were at being found. Then she snatched up the stack of menus from the floor where Brett had shoved them, and hurried right back out the door.

Silence stretched, filling the small office with it.

Kate stared at her hands. Well. At least her fountain of tears seemed to have dried up. What was left behind, however, was just as bad.

She could feel Brett watching her, but couldn't bring herself to look back at him. She was a Stockwell and

Stockwells didn't cry. They didn't pine. They didn't long for things they were too afraid to reach for.

She was a Stockwell.

But she was a coward.

Her heart was crying for more of his touch. Her body was demanding it. And he was so close she could smell the scent of the soap from his morning shower on his skin. But she still didn't, couldn't, make herself reach out to him.

She swallowed, folding her arms around herself. A coward. Utterly and completely. "I think we should—"

"Go," he finished flatly.

She swallowed. Nodded.

He didn't argue. Merely moved across to the door, movements almost stiff. He pulled open the door and waited, his expression as impenetrable as it had ever been.

Kate reached for her shoes too, wondering when on earth she'd pulled them off.

Probably when you were trying to climb into Brett's skin and stay there for good.

She rose abruptly, banishing the taunting voice inside her head. She didn't look at Brett as she slid past him and headed down the staircase.

They walked through the kitchen to the restaurant that was, if possible, even busier than it had been earlier. Tommy looked their way from where he was busy with a customer and sketched a wave as they passed through. Outside, Brett hailed a cab and they headed back to the hotel. She sitting on one side of the seat as far to the opposite of him as humanly possible. He, sitting square on his side, looking straight ahead. Only the rhythmic ticking in his jaw to show that he felt anything at all underneath his impassive expression.

Playing tourist had lost its appeal for both of them.

In the lobby of their hotel, Kate lingered. Looking toward the discreet gift shop. "I'll be up in a while," she told Brett.

He didn't protest. And she knew he wanted some distance just as badly as she needed it. She watched him stride through to the elevator banks. And then he disappeared from sight and she sank weakly onto the nearest cushioned seat.

She didn't know how long she sat there, encased in a sort of numb cocoon. Long enough for the concierge to walk over and ask if she needed assistance of some sort.

She thanked him politely for his concern and assured him she was fine. Assistance? No, she didn't need assistance. She just needed a life that wasn't based on lies and half-truths and lost dreams.

Hotel guests arrived and departed as Kate sat there. A flood of laughing men and women rolled through the lobby on a wave of noisy good cheer.

The podiatrists, she guessed wearily, watching the way they seemed to have an aura around them, binding them, pulling them together.

She'd never had that sort of camaraderie with so many people at once. Growing up, it had been her and her brothers. Add Brett to the mix. Hamilton, too. But mostly Brett. She'd had few close friends. Plenty of people she knew, of course. The Stockwells were known for their entertaining, their parties...like the Independence Day celebration when Madelyn Stockwell was supposed to have drowned on Stockwell Pond when Kate was just a baby.

But Kate had never felt alone, particularly. Not back

then. Because she'd had Brett. And then, she'd lost Brett.

She pushed herself up from the chair. The numbness was wearing off and she didn't like it one bit. She went into the elegant little gift shop and stared sightlessly at dozens of trinkets. Feeling empty inside, she paged through a magazine that she didn't buy. She turned to leave, only then noticing the display of children's clothes.

She reached for the small T-shirts proclaiming that they loved Boston. Her hands trembled as she unfolded first one, then another. Looking for the perfect size, the perfect colors for her niece and nephew.

Sunny yellow for little Becky.

Blue and red stripes for Rafe and Caroline's baby Douglas.

And matching little billed caps.

Plus shorts. Yes, the shorts completed the outfit. But only because the miniature-size socks were added to the mix as well.

She added them all to the pile, barely aware of the salesclerk carrying the selections to the counter where the cash register was located.

Little leather biker jackets.

And finally, two stuffed collectibles. A yellow turtle for Becky and a red one for Douglas.

She signed the chit and waited while the salesclerk found a bag large enough to contain all the items. And while she waited, she noticed a lovely gold pin that would suit Hannah. Then, of course, she found a perfect bracelet for Caroline. The clerk added the last two items to the bill, boxed them in their small leather cases and added them to the bag and handed it all to Kate with a satisfied gleam in her eyes.

Kate managed a smile, and carried the cumbersome bag through to the lobby and to the elevators.

There was no point in putting off going to the room any longer. Sooner or later she was going to have to face Brett. Face the past.

Seemed that was the focus of her life these days.

She believed Brett when he said that he'd tried to see her at the hospital. She believed him when he said that Caine had manipulated the situation to suit himself.

She even believed that he hadn't been dancing with Donna Lee Delatore at that endless wedding reception eight years earlier with anything more on his mind than not getting tripped up in Donna Lee's hideous, floor-dragging gown.

But knowing those things, believing them, didn't change the other, most basic facts.

Such as a mother who'd left her home and her children for reasons they still couldn't determine.

Such as a father who'd never had time for her, and when he did, it was only to serve his own selfish purposes.

And mostly, most importantly, the lover who'd put their relationship—put *her*—at the bottom of his priorities just as surely as her own father and mother had.

The elevator doors slid open and she stepped out on their floor, then, because her arms were so full with the weighty bag, she bumped her elbow against the door in a blunt-sounding knock.

It took only a few moments before Brett pulled open the door and looked down at her.

His eyes cooled as they focused on the oversize gift-shop bag. "I might have known," he said evenly. "Shopping. Kate Stockwell's cure for the world's ills. What'd you buy? Another dress you don't need?"

She jolted, as if she'd run smack-dab into the flat of his hand. "Yes, Brett," she answered, hating the shakiness in her voice. "Lots and lots of stuff I'll never need."

She dropped the bag on the bed and some of the miniature-size clothing tumbled out.

His gaze followed.

She ignored him and dropped her purse on the dresser.

He'd taken one hand to the bag and tilted it, causing the rest of her purchases to tumble out onto the foot of the bed.

"Baby clothes," he murmured. "For who?"

"My niece and nephew."

He looked again at the sizable array of items. "Playing the devoted aunt to the hilt, aren't you."

She smiled, not feeling one speck of humor in her soul. "That's me. Devoted Auntie Kate," she agreed flatly.

And why not?

Being an aunt was all she had. All she would ever be.

Because the one thing that Kate would never be—could never be—was a mother.

Chapter Thirteen

"Those kids are gonna grow up *really* loving their aunt Kate if you go around buying out the store every time you want to give 'em a gift," Brett said.

Kate lifted her shoulder and began gathering up the stuff that he'd just dumped out. She didn't look at him. "What does it matter to you? I can afford it."

"Never said you couldn't, Kate. God forbid anyone ever forget you're a Stockwell. That you can buy and sell most of the rest of us."

"I am also an ex-Orwell," she reminded in a brittle tone. "Don't want to forget that, now, do we? And my settlement from Hamilton was, if nothing else, generous." She shoved a stuffed animal into the bag. Then just as abruptly pulled it back out, as if to see whether she'd hurt the oddly cute little thing or something.

"Why? You guys were only married a few years." And every time Brett thought about Kate being another man's wife, it made something inside him freeze over. "What'd you do, Kate? Get bored being the trophy wife for good ol' Ham? Is that why you went back to school to learn how to delve into other people's minds, 'cause you didn't like what was going on in yours?"

Her hands crumpled over the edge of the bag and he cursed himself to hell and back for the cold, cutting question.

Again, her shoulder lifted. And it might have convinced him of her blithe unconcern for his words if it weren't for the fact that, right above the round neckline of her top, he could see her pulse visibly beating in her too-pale throat. "Does it matter? Nothing I say is going to make you hate me less."

"Hate? I wish to God it was that cut-and-dried."

She moved the bag to the dresser. "What do you want from me, Brett? Do you want me to say that I regretted marrying Hamilton the second we said *I do?* That our first year together was miserable because I could barely let him touch me without freezing up? That every minute of every day for months was a sheer effort to get through because I couldn't rid myself of thoughts of you?" Her voice broke. "Is that what you want, Brett?"

"I want the truth, Kate."

"Why?" She looked at him, her eyes wounded. "So you can beat me over the head with it? Well, beat away, Brett. It doesn't get more true than that."

He looked at her. Beautiful in her peachy-orange outfit that only emphasized the dark gleam of her hair and the golden cast of her taut shoulders and sleekly muscled arms. She was every inch "The" Kate Stockwell, from head to toe, and only the pulse throbbing in her neck and the bruised ocean-blue of her eyes, gave evidence otherwise.

And he had to acknowledge that when it came to expecting her to be ''The'' Kate Stockwell, he was just as guilty as everyone else.

He sighed heavily and sat on the foot of the bed, elbows propped on his thighs. ''What happened with Ham?''

''We divorced,'' she said flippantly.

His patience, shaky at best, was seriously strained. ''Why?''

''I don't want to talk about Hamilton.''

''Then why'd you bring up his name again?''

Her lashes swept down, hiding her eyes. ''Why were you in a bar fight here in Boston seven years ago? Drunk and 'stoned' on painkillers?''

''Because my ex-fiancé had just married my best friend and the bastard who'd fathered me had just died in a prison near here and I had the pleasure of seeing to the last details of his life just months after I'd finally found out who the hell he was.''

Her hand covered her mouth for a long moment. Then she slid to her knees in front of him, putting her arms around his shoulders, pressing herself against him. Warm and shaking and smelling like heaven. ''Oh, Brett. I'm sorry. I'm so sorry. But painkillers, Brett. What…?''

He put his hands on her shoulders pushing her back. Steeling himself against the wealth of compassion in her eyes. ''You weren't the only one hurt in the accident, Kate. What happened with Hamilton?''

Her brows drew together, her throat working. Her hands lifted toward him, palms upward. Beseeching. ''Brett, I don't—''

"I saw you leave the hospital with him, Kate. I waited in the parking lot and watched him help you from the wheelchair into his perfectly polished Mercedes." Ham's expensive car. So suited to the two of them. While Brett's secondhand truck had been barely shy of an eyesore. Until the accident. After that, it had been scrap metal and nothing more.

Brett let go of her shoulders and brushed his thumb over her temple. "Ham kissed you," he said. "Right there." He touched her cheek. "And there. I saw it all."

He dropped his hands.

Her own hands fell, too. "But that was two weeks after the accident," she said faintly. "Where were you staying? The apartment was empty. Jack said it was completely empty except for my things. Your clothes gone. Everything. Gone."

"It doesn't matter where I stayed," Brett said flatly. "I went to the hospital on the day you were released, because even though you'd dumped me—I'd believed that you'd dumped me," he corrected grimly, "I needed to see you. Make sure that you were going to be okay. I'd called the floor nurses and gotten nowhere. But there were a few stories in the newspaper about your recovery and when you were to be released." Mostly, however, they'd focused on Kate's arts degree, various works of hers that had already won awards, giving a hint of a promising career as an artist. And every time he'd read them, pored over the brief gossipy bits, he'd felt damned even more for not preventing the accident.

"Of course it matters where you were staying," she protested faintly. "You were hurt. Why else would you have been prescribed painkillers? Just tell me, Brett. Please. I—" She broke off. Swallowed. "I need to know that you weren't alone. That *someone* was taking care of you."

"I had a few busted ribs," he said shortly, remembering that he'd been very much alone. "My back was messed up some." Some. Enough that it still gave him fits on occasion.

The edge of her teeth closed over her lip. "Bad enough that you took painkillers."

He didn't see the point of answering that and he could see by the sad acceptance in her eyes that she recognized it.

She shifted, sitting with her knees drawn up and her back against the dresser behind her. She wrapped her arms around her knees, looking defenseless and very un-Kate-like. "Hamilton was there for me after the accident," she said after a moment, not looking at him. "He helped keep me going when I felt like I didn't have the strength to blink."

"He was there for you and I wasn't. That's what you believed."

She closed her eyes for a moment. "Yes."

Her answer sat there, between them. Painful. Raw. Truth.

She pushed one hand through her hair, leaving her palm pressed against her forehead. Shadows filled her eyes. "If our relationship hadn't been…shaky in the first place, I would have known better than to believe it no matter what my father did or said."

"There was nothing shaky about us, Kate."

Her shoulders moved. "Yes, there was. But I didn't know how to tell you that. You already thought I was, well, impetuous. I couldn't bring myself to tell you that I didn't know what I wanted out of life anymore, other than you. So I kept pushing about the wedding. Thinking that once we were married, I could make everything be okay.'' She went silent for a long while.

Brett didn't know what to say, either. When she did speak again, it shocked the hell right out of him.

''I, um, I thought I was pregnant.'' Her words sat in the darkening room, seeming to take on a throbbing life of their own.

''What?''

She breathed slowly. ''Before the accident.'' Her voice was husky. ''I was late. And I was afraid I was pregnant. On top of everything else I was feeling, it was just too much. That's why I wanted us to set the wedding date so badly.''

He froze even more. God. So simple. Yet it had never occurred to him. She'd been on the pill. They'd always been careful. ''Why didn't you just say so?''

She shifted. ''I did one of those home pregnancy tests,'' she whispered. ''It seemed like it read positive to me. And then I set an appointment with a doctor in Dallas, because I didn't want anyone in Grandview getting word that I was seeing an Ob-Gyn.''

''That doesn't explain why you didn't tell me.'' His chest ached. His head ached. He managed to keep his temper only through sheer effort.

''I didn't want a pregnancy to be the only reason you would marry me.''

''I loved you, Katy.''

She made a soft sound. ''I was scared. I wanted you to marry me for me, not because of your sense of responsibility.''

He sighed deeply. She was right about that, in a sense. If she'd been pregnant, they'd have been married right away. No matter how broke he was, or how much he'd felt like the pauper to her princess. "You weren't pregnant, though. Were you?"

Again that soft sound. He almost turned on a light so that he could see her expression more clearly.

"No," she said finally. "I wasn't pregnant."

He closed his eyes, relief coursing through him. If she had been pregnant, and the accident had harmed that, he wasn't sure what he would have done.

"I'm sorry, Brett. For so many things." Her hands lifted, then fell. "I shouldn't have agreed to marry Hamilton. It managed to ruin the friendship that we'd had. I did care for him, Brett. We were like the Three Musketeers once. Remember?" Her throat worked. "When we first moved to Houston, I thought things would be better there than they'd been in Grandview. And so did he. We did try. Only nothing was better. We were just living on a different street. And in the end there was no point in pretending. I wasn't…what he wanted. And he—" Her jaw twisted. "And he wasn't…you."

She drew in a quick breath and let it out. "He's married again. He and his wife have two children, last I heard. He's happy and I'm glad. They live in Phoenix, now."

"And you have your career, helping your kids with their troubles. Is that what you wanted, Katy?"

A wave of something crossed her face. Then she nodded. "Patients," she corrected. "And it is what I have," she said evenly as she pushed to her feet. Brushing away the wealth of pain in her eyes as surely as she brushed her hands over her hips, smoothing down her loose, flowing pants.

She looked around, seeming surprised that the room had fallen into shadow. That so much of the day had passed. It was early evening, and Brett knew with fatalistic certainty that if they stayed in the room together, they'd end up in bed together, despite the complications it would cause.

And for eight years, he'd been careful not to let complications mess with his world.

"Let's go to a movie," he said abruptly.

Kate's eyebrows shot up. She looked unsteady. Dazed. "What?"

"We need to get outta here. At least for a while." If she gave him so much as a hint of an argument, he was not going to be responsible for his actions.

"Right now?"

He nodded, telling himself that he was not so far gone that he was disappointed at not having a tearing good debate with her. "No time like the present."

She tilted her chin and picked up her purse. Closed herself in the bathroom for a few moments and came out, hair brushed into a smooth bell that grazed the peachy-melon shoulders of her top and the golden curve of her bare shoulders. Her lips looked moist and gleaming thanks to whatever dab of stuff she'd painted them with.

Oh, yeah. It was a good thing for them to get out of the privacy of the hotel room. Because, despite the revelations of the past few days, the differences between Kate and him were alive and well.

She was china. He was a foam cup.

The reasons they'd parted may not have been what he'd thought, but there was still no changing all the rest.

"Do I look okay?"

Brett's eyebrows rose. He put his hand over his cell phone for a moment. He was talking to his office, the way he had each morning. "You look beautiful. You always look beautiful, Kate."

Her lips twisted. And color touched her cheeks. "I just want to look nice."

She was all in white. From the delicate sandals wound around her feet in an interesting concoction of narrow little straps, to the sleeveless dress that clung to her svelte curves and swayed all the way down to her ankles. Nice was a puny word to describe the way she looked.

A gut-wrenchingly beautiful dark-haired angel might be closer to the mark.

"You look *nice,*" he assured. "But we're just going to see Marissa Deane, sweetheart. Not Madelyn herself. And it may not pan out," he added.

Kate nodded, fingers brushing through her hair. "I know. I know. I'm sorry. Finish your call." She was a bundle of nerves and had been pacing the length of the hotel room for the past half hour as they both watched the clock slowly tick toward 10:00 a.m., when the Marissa Deane Gallery was supposed to reopen.

She'd be hard-pressed, however, to say which was causing her nerves more trouble. The present Brett. The past Brett. The fact that they were nearing ever closer to Madelyn.

All were jumbled in her head, in her heart.

She nearly jumped out of her skin when Brett stepped next to her where she'd been staring blindly in the mirror. He'd finished his call and she hadn't even noticed.

"Come on," he said. "Let's go."

Her eyes flew to the clock on the nightstand beside the bed. "It's too early yet."

"Then we'll wait outside the door of her gallery. Come on, Kate. It's gonna be fine. You can do this."

She swallowed. Pulled in a shaky breath and nodded. "Right. You're right. Of course." She smoothed her hands down her dress. Lifted her chin and straightened her shoulders. "This is what I'm here for. Right?"

His eyes were suddenly unreadable. "That was the plan."

Kate looked away. She grabbed her little white crocheted purse and pulled open the door. Somewhere along the way, "the plan" had become irrevocably entwined with something else altogether. Something that began and ended with Brett.

They took a cab to the Marissa Deane Gallery. A trip that took too little time, because it seemed to Kate that they were standing on the sidewalk outside the brick-fronted gallery within the blink of an eye.

The sign that she'd grown used to seeing in the window was gone. And suddenly, Kate felt sick to her stomach. Until Brett's hand closed around hers. And just that easily, her nervousness eased to a tolerable level.

They walked across the sidewalk, and Brett tried the door, despite the fact that it wasn't even half past nine, yet. Locked.

"Maybe we should…I don't know. Have breakfast or something," Kate suggested. Then flushed when Brett's eyebrows rose as he looked at her.

"You're willing to eat finally?"

Truthfully, she didn't think she could swallow a bite. "You must be hungry."

"We'll both eat after we've talked with Marissa Deane." He jiggled her hand. "Come on. Let's walk."

So they walked. Up the block. Down the other side. Brett told her about a new case that had come into his office recently. Kate told him more about Bobby's case.

"Sounds like the father needs some counseling, too," he said.

"That would help, of course," Kate murmured. "He can't face the loss of his wife, and until he can, he's not going to be of much help to their son, but he's a young father and he won't buck his parents' belief."

"Maybe he had something to do with the mother's supposed suicide."

"I don't think so." She shook her head. "I even tried using the weight of the Stockwell name to influence the police chief into opening an investigation. It did no good, obviously."

"You really care about your kids, don't you."

"Patients. Yes. I do. I'm sure you care about your cases, too." She glanced up to realize they were standing once more in front of the gallery. And this time, the door was pushed open wide.

Brett was guiding her inside before she'd barely had time to react. Across the open space, illuminated by a soaring ceiling that was studded with skylights, a woman was standing behind a delicate desk, a phone at her ear.

She noticed them and smiled, giving a little wave of her hand to invite them further in.

Kate trembled and Brett's arm slid around her shoulder, holding her close against his side. Through his fine cotton shirt, she could feel his heat. And he gave her an encouraging wink.

Then the woman was hanging up and turning her pleasant expression their way. "Good morning," she greeted and gently waved her arm again, indicating the nearly empty floor space. A wide, expensive bangle bracelet on her arm reflected the shaft of sunlight from above. "Welcome to my gallery. I'd invite you to look around, but as you can see, there is nothing much to look at quite yet." She smiled again, her expression politely inquiring. "The crew that was supposed to help put out my inventory is running late."

Kate couldn't speak to save her soul. But Brett had no such problems. He introduced himself, and Kate— even though she'd gotten used to being introduced as his new wife over the past several days—felt her cheeks heat, now.

"Newlyweds. How lovely. I'm Marissa Deane. Are you honeymooning here in Boston, then?"

Brett nodded and got right to the point. "We understand that you may have some pieces by Madelyn LeClaire. And I'd very much like to add to our collection. As a wedding present for my bride."

"Well, I don't have as many LeClaire's as I'd have liked to have," Marissa admitted. "I had a fire, you see. About a month ago. Sadly I lost two." She tilted her head, her expression assessing. "You say you have a collection?"

"A small one." He smiled down at Kate with all the appearances of a besotted bridegroom and pulled out the snapshot of the painting. "We happened upon this in France. And, obviously, fell in love with it since the subject looks so similar to my wife. We'd heard that the artist might be represented out of Boston and hoped to find something before we have to head back home."

Marissa's eyes softened. "That's just lovely," she murmured. "And with your beautiful dark hair, I can see the similarities. Mrs. Larson, you're very lucky to have a husband who wants to please you so."

"Yes," Kate murmured, not entirely sure where the words came from. "I am very lucky."

"Well." The gallery owner brushed her palms together. "As it happens, I do represent the artist. And not everything was destroyed in the fire, thank heavens. But everything I have in my inventory is already sold and should have been shipped."

Kate's shoulders drooped.

"However, if you don't mind waiting, I'll go back and take a look just in case they didn't go out yet. That way, you could at least *see* one." She glanced from Kate to Brett and when they nodded, she strode, high heels clicking on the hardwood floor, through a door in the back.

Brett's fingers massaged Kate's shoulder. "Bingo," he murmured.

Kate didn't have time to respond before Marissa returned with a wide painting in her hands. She set it on a tabletop easel that she pulled from behind the desk.

And Kate swayed. Only Brett's body beside her held her steady. It was a coastal scene. A rough, sprawling stretch of beach, with the pale surf flowing up over the shore, so beautifully depicted that Kate could practically smell the salt of it. But it was the figure standing on the sand, staring out over the ocean that captured Kate's attention the most.

Daddy, was her first thought. But when her feet carried her, unthinkingly, closer to the oil painting, she could see the impression was just that. An impression. Perhaps it was Caine. Painted from Madelyn's memory. Or it might have been Caine's twin. Brandon.

Kate pushed her fingertips against her forehead, staring at the painting so fiercely that it made her hurt inside. She barely heard Brett's conversation with Marissa Deane, she was focusing so intently on the painting. Thinking about the woman who had painted it.

She had to be her mother. Didn't she?

It all made such terrible sense. Yet, Kate still found herself finding it difficult to believe.

"I can contact the artist, perhaps. I know she has been working on some new paintings. Possibly we could arrange for you to see them before you have to return to Texas."

Suddenly Kate focused on Marissa Deane's words as she talked with Brett. She turned around, resting one hand against the desk for support. Felt Brett's gaze touch on her, dark and steadying.

"That would be great," he told the art dealer. "Anything that puts us closer to another LeClaire. But I'm afraid our time here in Boston is limited."

"Why don't I see if I can get in touch with her right now," Marissa offered. She laughed softly. "I don't ordinarily make such offers. But, well, you just remind me so of my own husband. He made a similar, grand romantic gesture on our honeymoon." She glanced at Kate. "Feel free to sit down, my dear. You're looking a little pale. I won't be long." Then she headed back to that door in the rear of the room.

As soon as she was gone, Kate covered her face with her hands. The feel of Brett's arms coming around her was the only thing that kept her from embarrassing herself with a complete breakdown into tears.

"Come on, Katy. We're almost there," he murmured against her temple, his hands running soothingly over her back. "Show me a little Kate Stockwell, here, love."

He was right, she knew. She nodded. Swallowed. Scrabbled for composure with everything she possessed. And slowly stopped trembling. Managed to blink away the pressure behind her eyes, step away and lift her chin.

Saw the pride in his eyes and wavered again for a

long moment. But then they heard Marissa's footsteps again and they both turned toward the woman.

Her attractive face was split into a delighted smile. She extended a slip of paper toward Brett. "I spoke with Madelyn. She has offered to meet with you tomorrow morning at her home in Chatham. If you are still going to be in the area, that is."

"We'll make sure of it," he assured as he took the paper from the woman. "We really can't tell you how much we appreciate your help."

Marissa just smiled and waved away their thanks. "I get my commission one way or the other." She laughed lightly. "And truly, I wish you and your wife every happiness."

Then, as if on cue, her phone rang. A trio of men entered the front door, dressed in work clothes and carrying ladders.

Brett looked at Kate, his gaze giving her strength as they left the gallery. He held up the slip of paper that she could see contained an address, a phone number and some driving directions. "You up for a trip to the Cape in the morning?"

Kate knew she should be crowing with satisfaction.

Yet, knowing that she was finally within touching distance of having so many questions answered, all she felt were more doubts.

"Brett?" She looked up at him. Absurdly grateful for his presence. "Could we go somewhere today? Do something where I don't have to think and worry and wonder?"

His dark gaze seemed to see into her head. Her heart. And understand everything that she couldn't quite bring herself to say. "Yeah, Katy. We can do that."

Chapter Fourteen

They went to Cambridge. They didn't even stop back at the hotel to change clothes. They just went.

Once across the river, they stopped in a restaurant where Kate managed to do reasonable credit to her eggs Benedict before Brett polished off the remainder after he'd already eaten his own egg-smothered waffle.

They rented bicycles and rode around the campus at Harvard. Kate tucked her dress up around her knees so it wouldn't catch in the chain, and Brett rolled up the sleeves of his shirt.

They visited the Harvard Art Museums and argued over the merits of contemporary sculpture. They took in an afternoon matinee of an old movie, and they sat in a park and ate hot dogs while Brett tried—and failed—to figure out how the leather straps on her sandals worked.

Then they arranged for a rental car to use the next

day and Kate bought a local travel guide that gave a delightful running commentary about every mile between Boston and the Cape, and the town of Chatham that was located right on the elbow of it.

By the time they headed back to the hotel, Kate's nose was pink from the sun, and Brett's bronzed skin seemed even more so. And thanks to the way he'd kept her mind busy on other things, Kate had actually relaxed when she'd least expected to.

Well, that was the trouble with Brett. Or the fascination with Brett. Things were never quite as she expected. And the man he was now was as intriguing, if not more so, than the memory of the man he'd been.

In their room, the message light on the phone was flashing and Kate left Brett to deal with it while she closed herself in the bathroom for a quick shower. Each day they'd returned to messages from his secretary, Maria, on the phone. No doubt it was more of the same.

After Kate was done with her shower, she'd call the mansion to fill in her brothers on the latest news about Madelyn. And after that…well, she and Brett had already agreed to order in pizza again.

He wanted to retaliate on that win of hers in gin rummy.

Just thinking about it put a smile on Kate's lips. A smile that wasn't even dimmed when she realized that the robe she'd thought she'd left hanging on the back of the bathroom door, wasn't there after all. She merely wrapped herself in one of the voluminous white bath sheets and pulled open the bathroom door. Smiling faintly at the way the steam sort of billowed out in great puffs.

But when she came out of the bathroom to head for the closet where her robe must be hanging, instead, she found Brett standing beside the bed wearing a grim expression.

She went still. "Something wrong at your office?"

He blew out a rough sigh. "The message was from Cord."

Kate's fingers tightened around the knot holding her big bath towel in place. "What did he say?"

Brett's eyes met hers. And she knew. She knew with every fiber of her being. While she and Brett had been out, tramping around Cambridge to keep her mind off of what they'd be doing the next day, her brothers back in Grandview had been dealing with a trauma of another kind.

"Daddy," she said.

He nodded. "You should call and talk to your brothers. All Cord said on the message was that he needed to talk to you ASAP about your father. It could be something else, entirely, Katy."

Her suddenly shaking legs found the edge of the mattress and she sat down with a plop. "It's not something else," she murmured. Water dripped from her wet hair onto her shoulders, where it ran in cold rivulets down her chest to get stopped up by the folded-over edge of the towel circling her. "Can you hand me the phone?"

He did. And she dialed the mansion. Cord, himself, answered. As if he'd been waiting by the phone for it to ring. Perhaps he had been. "It's Kate," she said abruptly. "Daddy's gone, isn't he?"

"Kate. Yeah. Earlier today." It would have been hypocritical for them to pretend to feel overwhelming grief. And yet, Kate was aware that her brother's voice was as somber as it had ever been. And she knew he was feeling the same thing she was.

Sadness that things had been the way they were. Acceptance that things had been the way they were. And, maybe, some bit of resigned relief that it was over.

She closed her eyes for a moment. And nearly jumped out of her skin when Brett settled a second towel over her shoulders and arms. She cast him a grateful look and huddled underneath it, holding it together with one hand. "I should come home," she told her brother.

"It'll be a few days before we get the arrangements made," Cord said and she heard him sigh. "The service won't be until Sunday at the earliest. There's no point in you trying to rush back tonight or anything. You making any progress at your end on finding the art dealer?"

Kate rubbed the pain in her forehead. "Actually, yes. We found Madelyn's art dealer just this morning."

"You're kidding."

"No. I was just going to call you in a little bit, actually, when Brett said you'd left a message. There's more, Cord. Madelyn apparently lives in Chatham. On Cape Cod. She's agreed to meet with us."

"What? When?" Kate could practically feel her brother's astonishment.

"Well, she thinks we're just a couple who wants to acquire another LeClaire for our art collection," she said hurriedly. "She doesn't know my name at all. And we were going to drive down there tomorrow morning. But with Daddy gone now—"

"You're gonna stay there and follow through with Brett," Cord said immediately. "Kate, there is nothing you can do here. Trust me. But if you're that close to finding Madelyn, you've got to finish it, honey."

"But—"

"No buts, Kate. This is what we've been hoping for. Right?"

She sighed a little. "Right. If you're sure—"

"I could call a powwow with the rest, but there'd be no point. They'd all agree, Kate. Stay there. Hell, I wish I could fly out and be there in the morning to go with you. You and Brett have really found her."

"That was the plan," Kate murmured.

"Well, stick to it, Kate. Now, put Brett on will you? I've got a few things to go over with him."

So Kate handed the phone to Brett and she went back into the bathroom where she slowly dried her hair and pulled on a pair of drawstring pants and cropped top. She looked at herself in the mirror.

Thirty years old. With no parents to speak of.

Then she closed her eyes, giving herself a shake. Who was she to moan about her life? Brett's mother had died when he was only nineteen years old. She remembered the day well. As well as she remembered the memorial service, standing beside Brett while people who had known his mother expressed their condolences to him.

The Orwells had been there en masse. Kate's brothers, except for Jack who'd been out of the country, had been there. Caine, however, had been conspicuously absent.

And then Brett had learned about his father, the way he had.

Kate turned away from her reflection and went back out into the room. No. She really did not have any room to feel sorry for herself. Not when there were others who had so much more reason to feel pain.

Brett was still sitting on the side of the bed. He'd

finished speaking with Cord, obviously, because the phone was back on the hook. "You okay?"

She nodded.

"Still want pizza?"

"Yes."

"Good. 'Cause it's already ordered." His eyes were impossibly gentle. "But they warned me it was gonna be at least an hour or so before it came. You gonna cry?"

"Maybe."

He nodded slowly. "Everything will be all right, Kate."

She laughed sadly. "Why? Because the mighty Brett Larson says so?"

His head tilted. "Seems as good a reason as any. Seems to work for my mighty Katy."

She closed her eyes for a moment. *My* mighty Katy. So many inaccuracies in that. She wasn't his "my." She was so far from "mighty" it was laughable. And only to Brett had she ever been Katy.

When she looked at him again, his eyes, so dark, so brown, were gentle. He held up his hand. Just waiting.

Feeling as if she was standing on the edge of a precipice, Kate slowly took a step toward him. Put her hand in his.

And then he tugged her down onto his lap and put his arms around her, pushing one of his ever-present pristine handkerchiefs into her hand.

And held her. While she did cry.

And after she was all cried out, still he held her.

And Kate knew she had fallen in love with Brett Larson, all over again.

The knowledge seemed to flood her veins even as a

sharp knock on the door brought her head up from its resting place against Brett's wonderfully warm chest.

"Pizza," Brett said briefly and disentangled his arms from hers.

She dashed her fingers across her wet cheeks and rose, moving across to the table to clear it off and make room for the food. But when she was done and turned to see Brett, it wasn't the pizza delivery person standing there, but the concierge of the hotel.

Kate frowned, wondering what on earth he was doing.

But then the man noticed her and smiled widely. "Mrs. Larson," he greeted. "We've got that two-bedroom suite that you requested ready for you. Finally."

Brett slowly turned around to look at her, his face impassive. "Isn't that nice? *Honey?*"

Swallowing against the knot in her throat, Kate hurried over to the doorway where the two men were standing.

One smooth and satisfied at fulfilling one of his guests requests. The other, calm and quiet and much, much too still.

"Actually," she told the concierge, "we've decided to remain in this room. If you don't mind."

The man lifted his eyebrows. "Well, no, ma'am. Of course we don't mind. But I was given to understand that you were quite insistent—"

"I changed my mind," Kate said hurriedly. She didn't like the look of utter stillness that had settled over Brett. "Thank you, anyway."

The man shrugged. Wished them a good evening and turned and left.

Kate slowly pushed the door closed.

"Why did you turn him down?"

"Because the reason I wanted the larger suite in the first place no longer applies," she admitted on a rush.

"And the reason was…?"

"To put some distance between me and you."

"And you don't want to do that now."

Her lips pressed together. But what was the point in continuing to pretend? "No. I don't."

"You confound the hell outta me, Katy. Do you know that? I've spent most of the past decade *un*complicating my life and you just walk all over that."

She lifted her shoulder. "Sorry."

He snorted softly. "Right. I know you too well, Kate. Confounding and complicating was always just good sport for you."

Then a knock sounded on the door again. And this time, it *was* the pizza delivery boy.

She waited until they were seated at the table, with the pizza steaming up between them. "I didn't go around *trying* to confound you," she finally countered.

"No," he agreed. "It just seemed to come naturally to you. You were—are—Kate Stockwell. You just sort of expect the world to form itself to your specifications."

"Makes me sound wholly selfish."

"No, it doesn't." He polished off his slice in a few bites, then reached for another. "You were young. Hell. We both were. God. The arguments we used to have." He shook his head faintly.

"We always made up," Kate murmured. Except for that last time, she thought. But then she noticed Brett's expression. And knew immediately that he was not thinking of their last argument, nor the accident that had derailed the course of their lives.

"Making up with you was always good," he said. "Definitely no problems in that department."

It was silly, but her cheeks burned.

Then Brett cast her a long look. "So, Kate? You wanna have an argument?"

Her jaw dropped.

And then she laughed. And immediately felt awful for it. She pressed her hand to her forehead and looked at him. "I shouldn't be laughing."

"Because of Caine."

She sighed. Nodded. And withstood Brett's quiet, intent look.

"What do you think he'd expect you all to be doing right now?"

"Not be sitting here with you," she murmured. "That's for certain."

His lips twisted a little. "True enough."

She suddenly pushed out of her chair, reaching across the legs he'd stretched from his chair to the side of the bed, for the deck of cards she'd dumped on the bed when she'd cleared off the table for the pizza. "I don't want to think about this now," she decided. "Is that awful?"

Brett shrugged. "You're the therapist, Kate."

She was. But Brett's opinion, his insight, mattered greatly. "Well." She slid the slippery cards from the box and tapped the deck against the tabletop. "You still want a chance at redeeming your pitiful loss the other night?"

"I let you win, you know," he said blandly. "To help preserve your self-confidence."

She pushed the tip of her tongue against her teeth. "You did not. You're not that tenderhearted," she told him suspiciously. She *had* won, and she hadn't expected to.

He shrugged, as if it mattered to him not at all. "You'll never know now, will you."

She tapped the deck again. "I am sure Daddy would not approve of us playing gin rummy right now."

"We could play strip poker, instead," he deadpanned.

Kate chuckled. But then her eyes stung with tears again. Brett noticed, for he tossed his unfinished slice of pizza back in the box and reached across, stilling her hands where they were worrying at the cards.

"We'll play another time," he said quietly. "You don't have to keep up any kind of front with me, Kate. You're upset. You don't have to hide it. Not from me."

She was upset. About her father. About what would happen the next day when they met with Madelyn LeClaire.

And she was upset at finding herself feeling just as lost and frightened at thirty as she'd been at twenty-two, when she'd loved—and lost—this man.

She tapped the deck once more on the table. "Play to five hundred," she said huskily. "Penny a point."

Withstanding Brett's gaze was one thing. Feeling positively chilled when he removed his hand from hers was more than she could stand, and she trembled.

"Penny a point," he agreed slowly. He pushed aside the pizza remains and waited.

And gathering her composure, Kate shuffled the cards and dealt them. And she was grateful when it took all of her concentration to keep pace with him, when he, most assuredly, didn't show her any mercy with the cards.

The game, when it finally ended, was in his favor. By fifteen points.

He tossed the cards on the table and pushed to his feet, seeming to grimace as he straightened. "Don't forget now, Kate. Five hundred big ones. Small denominations. Don't want anyone tracing me because of those big bills."

Kate smiled faintly. "Brett?"

"Yeah."

"Thank you."

She heard him exhale. Then his fingers grazed over her jaw in a bittersweet glide. "No thanks needed."

Then he was heading stiffly toward the bathroom. "Go to bed, Kate. I'm gonna run some hot water over these bones for a while."

She frowned a little. And when he came out of the shower nearly an hour later, accompanied by a thick cloud of steam, she was still sitting there in the chair, her sketch pad open beside her on the table that she'd cleared of pizza debris and cards.

He wore a pair of gray sweatpants that hung almost indecently low on his hips and a white towel looped around his neck, and Kate nearly choked at the sight of him.

His expression didn't look pleased to find her still sitting there in the chair. "I told you to get some sleep."

"I was never good at listening to orders," she countered huskily.

"You're telling me," he murmured. "Listen, I didn't have a chance to tell you earlier that if you want I could have someone look into the situation with your patient. Bobby. Nose around, see if anything comes up that the police didn't find."

"You'd do that?"

He made an impatient sound. "Don't sound so surprised. Not every case we take on is financed by some wealthy family."

"I didn't say anything of the sort. I just never expected...I mean...thank you."

He shrugged off her thanks. She watched him run the towel roughly over his head, making his thick dark hair even more tumbled. Then he tossed the towel into the bathroom and hit the switch with a stiff movement that Kate recognized all the way across the room.

"Did you hurt your back in the accident, too? Is that what the painkillers were for? Or was it a more recent injury?" Goodness knows his business wasn't *all* centered around finding missing persons.

He'd gone still at her question. "Go to bed, Kate."

"You're in pain right now. I can see it from here."

His lips tightened, impatient. "Kate—"

"Another one of the things I studied was massage therapy, Brett. Come on. I can help you."

His jaw tightened. "I don't think you putting your hands on my body right now would be real wise, Katy."

"Why not? I wouldn't hurt you, Brett. I do know what I am doing."

"No," he said flatly.

She sat back, wincing at the fierce jab of pain that caused. "I just thought I could help you," she said quietly. "You've been helping me all this time, and I—"

"You wouldn't be helping me, Kate. Trust me. Not unless you're prepared for the consequences," he said flatly.

She frowned. "What consequences?"

"You could do your massage thing on this damned catch I get in my back about a hundred times every week. And that'd be just fine. Except once you touch my back, I'm gonna want you to touch the rest of me, too. And somehow, I just don't think you're ready for that. Not tonight, anyway.''

Kate stared. Tried to stave off the tantalizing images that immediately flooded her mind. But she couldn't.

''Hell,'' he muttered. ''*I'm* not ready for it. Sex with you was always great, Katy. But the aftermath, well, let's just say I'd rather give it a miss this go-round.''

Kate smiled stiffly even as something new and hopeful inside her withered and curled into a tight ball.

She watched Brett snatch a pillow off the bed and toss it to the ground on the opposite side of the bed. Then he stretched out on his back on the floor with an audible groan.

''You're not going to sleep on the floor?''

''Bed's too soft for me right now.'' His voice drifted over the bed, finality in his tone.

She didn't know whether to believe him or not. She sighed and reached once more for her sketch pad.

Chapter Fifteen

"This is it."

Kate didn't need Brett's announcement. They were sitting directly opposite a charming, garden-fronted house with an address that exactly matched the directions they'd received from Marissa Deane the day before.

She felt Brett look at her. "We're a few minutes early," he said, his dark eyes unreadable. "We could grab some coffee or something before we do this. Give you a little more time to adjust."

"No. I couldn't eat or drink anything to save my soul." On any other day, the drive through the picturesque town of Chatham, located right on the elbow of Cape Cod, would have never been enough to satisfy her. She'd have wanted to get out of the car and explore every single inch of the charming town.

But this wasn't any other day.

"Look at that rose garden, Brett. So lovingly tended. How could a woman leave behind her children, but tend flowers like that?" Her voice was hoarse. Barely audible.

"We don't know for certain that this Madelyn is your Madelyn," Brett cautioned softly.

Then they went silent as they both saw the movement in the rose gardens across from them. A slender woman, dressed in flowing green, came into view. She held a basket of roses in one hand and carried what appeared to be small clippers in the other.

Kate's hands, held together in her lap, twisted. "Oh my gosh," she breathed in disbelief. "Do you see—"

Brett covered her hand with his. "Kate, sweetheart, don't get—"

"She looks just like me," Kate whispered. "Her hair, her posture. Oh, God, Brett." Pain, wide as the ocean, engulfed her. "All those years, people told me how much I resembled my mother. But it was just words. Nothing real. And now to see it." She shook her head, words failing her.

"Time to meet her," Brett said and climbed out of the car. Sleeping on the hard floor had helped ease some of the knots in his back, but the drive from Boston had managed to put another one in it. He'd never felt this deeply about a case and he didn't like it. So the sooner it was over, the better.

He rounded the front to Kate's side, but when he opened the door, she just sat there. "Kate?"

Her face was pale. "I can't," she whispered.

Brett went still. "What?"

"I can't go up there," she said flatly. "I can't walk up to her as if she didn't leave me and my brothers to be raised by a man who wasn't fit to raise poodles.

She'll take one look at me and know I'm not some newlywed on a hunt for her paintings.''

He sighed. Knowing by the look on Kate's face that she wasn't going to budge. ''I can't drive away from this, Kate. I've got to finish the job you and your brothers hired me to do.''

She nodded, surprising him that she didn't argue. ''I'll wait out here,'' she said shakily. ''My brothers would expect you to finish. But I...I can't go in there, Brett. I'm sorry. I'm a coward, I know. But I...I just can't.''

He could see the edge of panic beginning to form in her eyes and he leaned down and brushed his lips over her temple through the open door. ''You're not a coward,'' he assured softly. ''Are you going to be okay waiting out here?''

Kate nodded stiffly. ''Just get this over with, Brett. I'll be fine.''

Brett wasn't sure. But he was aware that they'd probably been noticed by the woman across the street, clipping roses outside of her quaint home. He straightened. ''Okay.'' He turned to head across the street.

''Brett?''

He paused, looking back at her. Feeling something crack inside him at the naked vulnerability in her face. ''Yeah?''

Her lips worked. And her eyes were glittering with a sheen that was painful to see. ''Thank you. I couldn't have gotten through this without you.''

He sighed deeply. Brushed his finger down her nose. ''I won't be long.''

Kate nodded. And watched him stride across the street, stepping through the gate, and then walking right up to Madelyn LeClaire. She heard his deep voice as he greeted her.

As he greeted Kate's *mother*.

She closed her burning eyes, unable to watch a minute longer, and sank lower in her seat, trembling wildly. As if it were the middle of a Texas winter, rather than a warm, humid seaside day. The next time she looked— unable to keep herself from doing so—neither Brett nor Madelyn were in the garden.

And Kate's eyes burned all over again as she focused on the beautiful roses. The lovingly tended house with the beach stretching right out from behind it.

So terribly, terribly different than the cold confines of Stockwell Mansion while she'd been growing up.

How could her mother have left them the way she did?

Oh, dear God, if she'd ever been able to have the children she'd wanted so desperately, Kate would have died before being separated with her own flesh.

She turned away again. Unable to look upon that fairy-tale-looking home one more minute. She had no idea how much time passed.

But suddenly, when she couldn't not look again, there was Brett. Striding across the narrow street, a flat wrapped parcel under his arm. His eyes searched hers as he stopped next to her side of the car and put the painting—it couldn't be anything but, considering the size and shape—in the back seat.

Then he rounded the car and climbed behind the wheel. He handed her a slender bottle of water that she took automatically. "It's her," Kate said flatly. "Isn't it?"

He pushed the key in the ignition and started the car. "Yeah. It's her. There's no doubt in my mind, Katy."

His gaze, so dark, so beautiful, rested on her. "I don't know whether to tell you I'm sorry, or to celebrate with you. But Madelyn LeClaire is most assuredly Madelyn Johnson Stockwell."

"Did you tell her?"

"No. You guys hired me to find her. Not surround her and demand answers or resolutions. What you do with the information now, is up to you. She thinks just exactly what Marissa Deane led her to think." His eyes focused on the water bottle in her hands. "She wanted to know if you were all right, seeing as how you stayed in the car. I told her you weren't feeling well from the drive. She thought you might like some water."

Her face paled even more. Her fingers tightened around the bottle. "Take me back to Boston, Brett." There was nothing so much as an order in the words. Nothing but a plea. And Brett barely contained the need to pull her into his arms and comfort her. Instead he put the car in gear, and headed back toward Boston.

Kate didn't speak much during the entire drive. He started to tell her about his conversation with Madelyn, but she shook her head and stared woodenly out the side window. She held the water bottle the entire way, though she didn't even attempt opening it. "I'll wait until my brothers can hear the information, too," she said unevenly. "That way you'll only have to go through it once."

Brett could have gone through it twenty times. But Kate's misery was palpable. His foot pressed harder on the gas. And they continued driving. In silence.

When they reached the hotel, Brett pulled the wrapped painting out with one hand, and Kate with the other. She let go of his hand, however, way too soon as far as he was concerned. "I'll be in the room," she told him in that husky, frozen tone that worried him.

He tossed the keys to the concierge, along with a handful of crisp bills, and caught up with her in the lobby. She didn't look his way on the elevator ride up, nor did she look his way when he unlocked the door to their room and preceded him inside.

"I have to call my brothers," she said dully.

"I'll do it." All he needed was for her brothers to hear her in the state she was in. They'd either string Brett up by his thumbs and leave him for the scorpions to finish, or they'd be on the first plane to Boston to charge after her. Neither option was particularly acceptable.

She nodded, without comment.

Brett laid the wrapped painting on the bed and went straight for the phone, keeping one eye on Kate. She stood in front of the painting for a long time, her expression pained. Then she set the water down and walked, stiff and awkward, over to the glass door. She pushed it open and stepped out onto the balcony just as Cord answered the phone at the mansion.

Brett relayed his information, rapidly. Concisely. And he listened as Cord told him what arrangements had been made for Caine's services. He absorbed it, but his attention was mostly on Kate. Watching her move on the minuscule balcony.

When he hung up with Cord, he called Maria, his secretary, and told her to get them on an early flight out the next morning. She promised to get on it, right way.

"Maria," he said, just before she had a chance to hang up. "Seat us in first class."

If she was surprised, he didn't wait around to hear it. He hung up and moved toward the balcony.

The angelic white that Kate had worn yesterday had been replaced by black, today. Flowing black slacks, the kind she seemed to wear a lot—that cinched her narrow waist with a drawstring and skimmed her hips, were topped by a sleeveless turtleneck sweater that clung to her womanly curves.

Brett had finally realized that the clothing she chose to wear was like an advance mood-indicator. Her hair was pulled back into a ponytail, and she looked removed. Untouchable. And so vulnerable that he just wanted to take her away where nothing would ever hurt her again.

He looked from the back of her to the painting sitting on the bed. Kate hadn't displayed one breath of curiosity over it. Another sign that she was closing herself off.

He sighed, scrubbed his hand down his face and stepped out to join her. "Maria's getting us seats on an early flight tomorrow."

She didn't answer.

He touched her elbow. "Kate? Did you hear me?"

Her eyes slowly lifted to his. "Make love to me," she said abruptly. Her voice was raw. "Make love to me now, Brett. Right now."

His gut tightened, all semblance of peace or quietude disappearing in a fiery instant. "Kate—"

"Please, Brett."

His eyes closed. His jaw was suddenly so tight it ached. "Dammit, Kate. Don't do this to me. To yourself. You're upset. Now's not the time."

"Then when *is* the time? I thought you wanted me."

"I do."

"Then make love to me. Help me forget…for just a while."

"Forget what? The past? The future?"

Her eyes filled and he felt like the bastard he was.

"Forget that nobody really needs me," she said painfully.

"For God's sake, Kate. You don't exist as a reflection of other people's needs!"

"And you never *cared* enough about anyone to share your needs! You...you're as bad as all the rest," she flared. "You claimed to love me, but we both *know* that your career came first. Even now, you're here because of a case. Because of your *career*." She flinched as the words came out of her mouth. She stepped back inside the room.

"We're back to that, now? Money." He followed her. "I worked hard when we were engaged so that I could provide for *you*, Kate. For our future. Because I loved you. But you never wanted to understand that, did you!"

"I didn't need your financial support, Brett. I needed *you*. And you didn't need me. Pure and simple. You won't let yourself need *any*one."

"So you turned around and married Hamilton, instead. Well, Kate. Did he *need* you like this?" Brett's mouth came down on hers. Sheer force. Sheer fire. And it left her swaying when he lifted his head. *"Did he?"*

Then his hand swept down from her neck over her breast. Cupping her boldly in his palm. "Did you need him? Like this?"

She trembled wildly. "No," she choked. "You know I didn't."

"I don't know anything, Kate," he denied flatly. "Except that I want you worse now than I ever have before. But nothing's changed. I work for a living, Kate. I like what I do. It's who I am. And I'll be damned if

I'll get involved with you again only to have you look at me as if I'm cheerfully cutting out your heart because I am not prepared to spend every single waking minute with you while living off your family's money,'' he gritted.

She reeled. "I never—"

"I loved you, Kate. From the time we were barely teenagers. But I am a man. And I needed to provide. You never understood that."

"We were young," Kate whispered. "I understand it, now, Brett. I do. I don't want to change you. I'm not asking for anything beyond today. I know we had our chance. And it's gone. I know that."

"So you're willing to settle for a little slap and tickle for now?" he asked harshly.

Her hand flashed out and he caught her wrist in the bare second before her palm connected with his cheek. She stared at him, horrified at what she'd nearly done. Anger and fear and tension left her in a dizzying flood, leaving only a bone-deep ache in its wake. "I just didn't want to feel alone. For a while." Her teeth caught her lip. "That's all. Just for a while."

She turned away, wiping her cheeks. Humiliation burned. "I'm sorry I've offended you."

She heard his muffled oath. And then he pulled her around to face him. "There you go again, missing half of what I say," he muttered and yanked her into his arms, his mouth covering hers. Hot and hard and devastating.

Her heart threatened to jump out of her chest. His hands were on her face, holding it still, his eyes burning over her with an unholy golden gleam. "I want you, Kate. To my back teeth with it. One time is not going to be enough. A dozen times is not going to be enough.''

She felt utterly exposed to the intensity burning inside him. She exhaled and heard his name in it.

His jaw flexed and he moved the painting from the bed to the table. ''You were right about something, though. We *were* kids before. And we couldn't handle what was between us—for a lot of reasons—and we blew it. But I'm not a kid now and neither are you.''

''What are you saying?''

''I'm saying that you want to be lovers again. Fine. But that's where it ends.''

She stared. Slowly blinked. His shirtsleeves were rolled partway up his strong forearms and his thick hair was tumbled. As if someone's fingers had been tangling in it.

Her fingers.

''Have an affair,'' she whispered. ''That's what you mean.''

''No. Not an affair. That implies a beginning and an end. Hearts and flowers. I'll be your lover, Kate. No end in sight. But I'm not interested in marriage. We've tried going down that road once and it damn near killed us both. We're from different worlds. Foam cups and china just don't mix together.''

''I don't want to marry you, either,'' she said faintly. Even as she said the words, she knew she was lying. She wanted it all with Brett. But she knew, oh how well she knew, that her ''all'' was not enough for any man.

And maybe it was wrong of her, but all she could think about right now was being in his arms. Being so close to him that wrongs and rights, being smart and sensible, ceased to matter.

''Well, Kate? What's it gonna be?''

She moistened her lips. "I said it before, Brett." Her throat felt tight against the dizzying speed of her heart jumping up there. "Make love to me."

He stared at her.

And though she was trembling wildly, and a huge part of her wanted to retract the words, she didn't. She couldn't.

Slowly, wondering where she found the nerve, she reached for the hem of her sweater and tugged it over her head, letting it fall from her numb fingers to the carpet beneath their feet.

His lips tightened. His eyes narrowed.

Maybe they'd talked about being "just lovers" but the air was suddenly thick between them, redolent of something else entirely. Something wrapped up in the past, and wishing for the future, but standing there, large as life, right in the present.

Kate stepped out of her shoes. Losing two inches in height and feeling ridiculously small and female in the face of his tall, broad masculinity. And she hesitated, then. Assailed by sudden nerves.

He saw it. But instead of using it against her, turning it around in this battle of wills going on between them, he didn't. His expression seemed to soften and he reached out, tucking his hand behind her neck and tilting her head back for his lips.

He kissed her, softly at first. So softly and sweetly that she felt tears collect in her eyes at the beauty of it. He lifted his head, staring at her. Rubbed his thumb over the tear that had escaped.

She stepped into him, wrapping her fingers in the fine weave of his dress shirt. She didn't know where the sob that rose in her throat came from, she only knew that when it rose, he murmured and swept her up against him, holding her tight and safe.

"Are you sure?" His words were warm against her ear. "Be very sure, Katy, 'cause once I start I'm not gonna stop."

Her hands curled against his scalp, luxuriating in the feel of his heavy, silky hair. "I am sure. I don't want you to stop," she said quietly.

He exhaled roughly and stroked his palm down her spine, setting off a host of shivers. His mouth found hers and what had before been tender and gentle was suddenly filled with a raw, scorching heat.

Kate trembled wildly, her head falling back. A moan rose in her throat and an answering sound came from him. She swallowed, moistening her lips. Her breasts lifted and fell against the soft black lace of her bra with each unsteady breath her lungs drew.

"Take down your hair," he said softly, his expression so intense that it made her dizzy.

She reached up and pulled the elastic from her ponytail and her hair slid down to her shoulders. His hands sank into her hair, fingers twining in the strands. The ponytail holder slipped from her fingers, unnoticed. He tugged her head back, exposing the line of her throat for the burning heat of his lips. She swayed, catching his shoulders for balance.

The straps of her bra slid down her shoulder, aided by the seductive graze of his teeth against her skin. Then his mouth was on hers again, his taste hers, his breath hers. Her fingers dragged at the buttons of his shirt, popping one right off in her haste.

She felt his lips curve against his. "Impatient?"

She yanked at the lapels, pressing her breasts against his chest. "Yes."

He laughed softly, and with one hand, reached down to toss back the bedclothes. "Some things never change," he murmured.

Kate flattened her palms against the hard satin of his chest and exhaled shakily at the feel of his heart leaping against her touch. Her knuckles grazed his abdomen as she curled her fingers around his belt buckle, sliding it free. Then she reached for the zip, but his hand suddenly covered hers, stilling the motion.

She looked up at him, seeing the muscle ticking in his jaw, the heat in his eyes. "What?"

But he just shook his head once, and settled his hands on her shoulders, running them down the lace edge of her bra. Finding the center clasp and flicking it free, peeling back the lacy cups as if he were unwrapping a precious gift.

His hands covered her and she sank her teeth into her lip, her hands shaking so badly that she couldn't manage his zip. Brett drew her hands to his chest and pulled her close. Her curves fitting perfectly against him. He swept his hands down her spine, easily pushing her drawstring pants down her hips, leaving her standing there in nothing but a brief stretch of black lace.

She heard his breath hiss between his teeth and gasped when he suddenly tipped her off her feet and settled her in the middle of the wide bed. His eyes locked on hers, he finished undressing. Standing over her, looking so impossibly male, so impossibly beautiful, that it stole her breath.

She closed her eyes for a long moment, loving him so much that she wasn't sure she could contain the words. But his hands settled on her ankles and she felt him gently tugging her closer to the side of the bed. Closer to him.

He leaned over her, one hand on the mattress, one hand settling flat on her abdomen. She trembled madly, staring up at him, wanting so much, yet unable to so much as speak.

"You're beautiful," he murmured as he slowly, deliberately, guided her panties down her hips. She arched sharply and cried his name when he kissed the flat of her belly.

Her fingers clutched his shoulders. His neck. Sank into his hair and tugged. Lifted her head toward his, found his mouth. "Please," she begged. Her legs moved restlessly against his. "Don't tease me, Brett. I can't bear it."

"What do you want, Katy?" His words sighed over her jaw.

Unbearably maddened, she twisted her head, seeking his mouth. "I want you, Brett."

And at last, oh yes, at last she felt him against her, nothing between them but their skin, and even then it didn't seem to be anything at all. A sob rose in her throat as he pressed her back into the bed, even as he kept from taking her.

"You remember our first time, Katy?" His words whispered over her.

"Yes."

"We thought we'd never be with anyone else."

She closed her eyes and he thumbed away the tear that streaked its way down her face.

"We were," he went on, after a moment. "But nobody was you, Kate. It didn't matter how many years passed, nobody was you."

"Oh, Brett." She ached. She wrapped her arms around his shoulders. His hand glided along her side, flattened over her abdomen and slowly crept upward.

He cupped her breast and she bit her lip to keep from crying out.

Her legs shifted restlessly. Impatiently. And he laughed softly, utterly male, as he continued to madden her with his here-and-gone touches. Soft and slow and sweet. Hard and fast and raw. All of it was in his touch. All of it.

And when she was practically insensate with need, when her fingers were scrabbling at his shoulders, tugging, pulling him to her, because she couldn't bear the distance that was still between them, she felt him back away for a moment, then return. And the soft crinkle of that foil package sounded loud and intrusive.

She looked at him, at the protection he held between his fingers. And was grateful, oh so grateful that the afternoon sun had finally passed, that the room was in shadow. Because she'd never felt so exposed in all her life as she did right that moment.

"We don't need that," she whispered.

"Katy, I'm not going to take chances with you."

The emptiness yawned wide and bleak but she turned her back on it. "There's no chance. We don't need it," she said again. And then she reached for him, reveling in the hiss of his breath between his teeth. "I don't want anything between us. Not even that," she begged softly, her mouth searching for his. "Make me forget everything but you. But this moment."

Brett's control was dwindling. Kate was like a fever in his blood and she always had been. But now, now she was speeding over him with the ferocity of a tornado packed in a slender, perfectly formed female. He grabbed her hands and pressed them to the mattress. Looking down into her face. Her hair, spread out in a rich brown halo, her cheeks flushed, her eyes feverish sapphires, her mouth swollen and parted as she sucked in air just as desperately as his own lungs were.

"Oh, Brett." Her words whispered over him. "Don't make me wait any longer. It's been so long. Please." She lifted her head and touched her mouth to his, and his control just slipped through his fingers like grains of sand as he gathered her to him and made them one.

And when he did, he knew that he'd been the one believing the biggest lie of all. Because making love with his Katy was like going home. Finally.

She was sobbing his name and her arms, her legs were the sweetest bonds. It was like nothing else in this world.

And when she flew apart in his arms, he flew, too.

Chapter Sixteen

Kate felt Brett leave the bed early the next morning and closed her eyes against the feeling of abandonment that swiftly accosted her. She hated feeling that way, but seemed powerless to stop it.

So she tossed back the sheet that Brett had drawn over them at some point in the middle of the night, after they'd yet again driven each other to oblivion and back. If things had been different between them, if she had more to offer him than the temporary pleasure found in each other, she'd follow him into the shower that even now she could hear hissing through the wall.

But she didn't have more to offer.

Not that Brett had asked, anyway.

She grimaced, and reached for the first piece of clothing she could find. It just happened to be Brett's button-down shirt. She sniffed tearfully and pulled it on, then efficiently began packing her suitcase.

When Brett finally came out of the shower, feeling none too peaceful himself, it was to find the room painfully neat. The only thing out of place was the painting, sitting unwrapped on the dresser.

The sight of the woman wearing his shirt ought to have been out of place, considering everything, yet she wasn't. And it twisted at his gut, because he knew that they were simply too different.

"Guess you decided to look at the painting after all." He finished pushing down the knot of the towel around his hips. Kate still had a piece of the brown wrapping paper clenched in her hand. Her head slowly turned from where she was eyeing the painting. In the light from the bedside lamp her eyes looked like pools of agony.

"You're upset."

"Upset? Why would I be upset?" She waved her hand over the painting. "Look at them, Brett. It could be a painting of Caine and me. Except that my father never looked at me like that man looks at that girl. Brandon, I assume. And my…sister." She folded her arms tightly around herself, but he could see her shaking. "My mother never painted a portrait of *me*. She never painted a portrait of my brothers. No. She left us in that house with that…man. With Caine."

Her eyes glistened. "If she didn't want to stay with my father, fine. But why couldn't she have taken us, Brett? Why leave us there in that cold house with a man who didn't know how to feel for anything but his precious business!"

"You'll have to ask her that, Katy."

"And what? Find out just how little we mattered to her? I already know that." Her voice was brittle. "What is it about me, Brett? Why am I always last in the lives of the people I love? Daddy. M-Madelyn. You. Even Hamilton turned away from me.'' Her throat worked.

''You're not last, Katy. Stop thinking that way.''

''Can't stop the truth. It always has a way of coming out. I was a decorative daughter for Caine. A mere instrument in forging his alliance with a Supreme Court Judge. Madelyn. Oh, Madelyn is even more cut-and-dried. She just walked out.''

Brett thought again of the shadows in Madelyn's eyes that not even her serene expression had been able to counter. He beat down the urge to pull Kate into his arms and cradle her against him. ''Kate...about Madelyn. She's not what I expected. She's a beautiful woman. But there is something in her eyes. I don't know. A shadow, I guess. Old pain that dwells inside her.''

Kate's head shook back and forth, clearly not wanting to hear.

''That *is* Brandon,'' he confirmed quietly. ''While I was in the house talking with Madelyn, I saw him sitting on a chair outside the back. He was looking out at the ocean. I couldn't see all of his face—he was wearing sunglasses—but he was a Stockwell, Kate. He's as much like Caine as Rafe and Cord are like each other.''

Her fingertip reached out and trembled over the brush strokes of the portrait. ''My father never had this look in his eyes,'' she whispered faintly. ''This man—my uncle...Brandon...he knows what it is to love. You can see it in his face.''

''He and your mother are married.''

''My mother,'' she repeated, barely audible. Her fingers moved to the other person in the painting. ''And my sister.''

''Her name is Hope.''

Suddenly Kate crumpled. Her knees gave and if it weren't for Brett's arm around her, she'd have sunk to the ground. "Oh, baby, come on," Brett lifted her against him. "It's going to be fine. You're going to have your family, Katy. Soon."

"No." She shook her head. Her face was so pale, her eyes looked like blue bruises. "I'll never have a family. Not like the one I want."

"Why do you say that? Your brothers all dote on you. You know where Madelyn is now, and a whole new relationship may come out of that. How much more of a family do you want?"

"I want what we used to dream about when we were teenagers." She pulled out of his arms so rapidly that she knocked the painting right off the dresser. "I want children!"

"And you'll be a great mom." With some other man—a suitable man—as the father. The thought was the worst kind of bitter pill. "You'll find a guy from the china set and settle down with a passel of kids."

"You don't understand."

"Understand *what?*"

"I can't have children!"

He stared stupidly. "What?"

Her lips compressed. "I'm barren. I cannot have children."

"Why not?" He sat on the edge of the bed, feeling dead inside. "It *was* the accident, wasn't it? You were hurt more than I ever knew."

"It wasn't the accident! Would you stop dwelling on that bloody accident?" She pressed her fingertips to her temples. "I had endometriosis. And I didn't even know it until I went in for an exam when I was with Hamilton." Her lips twisted. "I was one of the rare cases that didn't experience the typical symptoms. But by the time it was diagnosed, it was too late. The condition was too advanced.''

He rubbed his hand down his face, swearing inside. Kate had always wanted children. He dropped his hands and looked at her. "I'm sorry. Is that what your nightmares are about?"

She frowned. "I...no. And you can save your pity. I don't want it."

"Good. You don't have it. For Pete's sake, Kate, can't you even accept some sympathy from me?" He pushed to his feet, anger filling him for reasons he couldn't begin to decipher.

"I don't want your sympathy, either."

"No, all you wanted from me was a roll in the hay."

She paled even more. "How can you say that?"

"Because it's true. You and me, Kate...we're impossible together. We're too different."

"Because you're this—" she waved her hand "—foam cup that you keep referring to? Come off it, Brett. Call yourself whatever you want, but we both know that you're not some cheap, flimsy piece of insubstantial foam. You don't want a future with me, fine. But you might as well let go of that self-image you've got. Nobody sees it but you. And maybe I should remind you that *china* breaks and is useless afterward, just like me. So being foam is quite often preferable!"

"You're not useless."

"I cannot have children!"

"I heard you the first time. Does that make you less of a person? Less of a sister, or a daughter, or an art therapist?"

Her shoulders sagged, as if all the fire had gone out

of her. "It made me less of a wife. Men want their wives to give them children. Pure and simple."

"You have scientific evidence to back that up?"

"I've got a divorce to back that up."

"If Ham left you because you couldn't get pregnant, then he was the useless one, wasn't he?" Brett said tightly. He reached for her, but she was as skittish as a colt, evading him.

"He said it didn't matter. My inability to conceive. He *said* it didn't make me less of a person. Yet when he got his mistress pregnant he couldn't get out of our marriage fast enough so he could marry her!"

"He was unfaithful to you?" Fury filled him.

"It doesn't matter."

"Everything about you matters."

She shook her head, denial written in her every pore. "We both agree that there is no future for the two of us together, so let's just drop this whole thing." Her voice was raw but she stepped back when he reached out a hand toward her. "I have to take a shower. We'll need to leave for the airport soon."

She strode past him and shut the bathroom door with a final snap.

It was like listening to a door slam on his soul.

When their plane touched down on Texas soil, Kate wanted to weep with relief. Beside her, Brett was pushing a notepad back into his briefcase. She could feel him looking at her, but couldn't find the courage to look back. She didn't think she'd ever been this tired, this heart-weary, in her life.

They exited the plane and silently walked through the bustling airport to the garage where his car was still safely parked. Kate cast around for something to say, something to alleviate the tense silence between them, to no avail.

And then they were driving, the top down again, the wind in her hair, and still she didn't manage to utter a coherent thought. Not even when he finally pulled to a stop in front of the mansion and pulled her suitcases and the painting of Brandon and Hope—rewrapped in padding and paper for the flight—from the car.

He carried everything up the wide steps, looking tall and broad and strong and beautiful.

She chewed the inside of her lip, halting beside him. But she couldn't meet his eyes. "Do you, want to come in?"

He looked out over the grounds, his expression unreadable. "I need to get to the office."

She nodded faintly. "Right. Of course." If nothing else had come of their time spent together, Kate knew she was no longer jealous of the dedication he gave to his work. "I know my brothers will want to hear about Mad—about our mother."

"I'll call. Set up a meeting, give them a full report."

She swallowed. Nodded. Scraped the toe of her shoes—the ones she'd bought that day in the department store with Brett—across the step beneath her. "Thank you."

She heard his faint sigh. "For what?"

Her throat tightened. "Letting me go with you. I know you didn't have to agree, no matter what I said. But it was important to me."

"To feel useful. And needed."

She looked down. "Yes. I know I didn't provide any real help, though. But I still appreciate it."

"You were the one that insisted we check out Maldovan,'' he reminded. ''I'd crossed them off the list. But he gave us our lead on Marissa Deane.''

''Well.'' She moistened her lips. ''It's nice of you to give me that credit.''

''It's not nice. It's the truth.''

''Well,'' she said again. Silence thickened between them, and Kate wondered why they couldn't hear the sound of her heart cracking. ''I'd better get in, too. I haven't called my office in two days.''

''What are you going to do about Bobby?''

''Try again,'' she said after a moment. ''See if I can make headway with his father to let Bobby reenter my program.''

''I meant what I said, Katy. About nosing around into the mother's death. If you want help there, just say the word.''

Tears ached behind her eyes. She was probably breaking some kind of ethical standard, but she didn't care just then. She couldn't fail that sweet boy. ''His name is Bobby Morales,'' she said huskily. ''I'll get his address to you later.''

Brett's lips stretched into a half smile. ''Okay. Good.'' He handed her the painting and she tucked it under her arm. ''Kate—''

She shook her head. ''Don't. I know what you're going to say. What happened last night…we're not meant to continue like that, Brett. You know it as well as I do. Let's just, just chalk it up to the past.'' To the goodbye they hadn't exchanged eight years earlier.

''I do care about you, Kate.''

Care. Not love. And certainly not need. She managed a smile and wondered why having her heart broken now seemed to hurt so much more than it had all those years ago. ''Me too.'' She pushed open the door and set the painting inside, propping it against the closed half of the door. Then she turned back and reached for her bags.

Her fingers brushed Brett's.

"I'll carry them up for you," he said.

"I don't think that's a good idea."

He let go and she firmed her grasp on the straps.

"I'll make sure you get that address." She turned toward the opened door, but froze when Brett's hand slid against her jaw. He smoothed his thumb along her cheek.

He leaned over her, his breath a warm caress on her temple as he pressed a kiss to her forehead. "Don't close yourself off from life, princess, just because of what you can't have. You have so much to give."

A hot tear slid down Kate's cheek, but Brett didn't notice.

He'd already turned and was striding down the steps to his car.

"So Madelyn LeClaire really is our mother." Cord stood in the center of the sunroom at the mansion, his arm around Hannah. "There is no doubt, anymore."

Hannah pressed her cheek to his shoulder, murmuring softly and Kate watched her brother run his hand along her pretty brown hair. She crossed her legs and looked away. Only to have her gaze fall on Rafe, who was standing closely behind Caroline, his arms looped around her shoulders.

"There is no doubt," Brett said. He'd brought in the painting of Brandon and Hope and it now sat propped on a side table. "She's settled in Chatham. She has no idea that I was anything other than a guy wanting to procure a painting for my wife. She's not going to bolt. The woman is *settled.*''

''What's she like?'' Hannah asked curiously.

Brett's gaze drifted to Kate and she suddenly felt like her skin was too tight. ''She's beautiful,'' he said evenly. ''A little gray in her hair. A few inches shorter than Kate, but they could be sisters as easily as mother and daughter.''

Kate swallowed and looked down at her hands.

''And she looked happy,'' Jack said quietly.

Brett nodded. ''Yeah. We spoke for about an hour. She talked about her husband and her daughter.'' He glanced at Kate for a moment, then he looked back at the other Stockwells.

He'd come to the house to attend the private funeral for Caine, knowing that he'd be meeting with the family afterward to share his findings. And he'd known that Kate would naturally be there.

He hadn't known that she'd work like a demon to pretend that he was invisible. All during the funeral service; the brief amount of time after, when the few non-Stockwells were expressing condolences and leaving; and now.

It annoyed the hell out of him, but he was hard-pressed to know what to do about it. He couldn't be just her lover, but he knew just as well that there was no future for them.

''So we know where she is, finally,'' Rafe said. ''We just don't know *why.*''

''She needs to know about Caine's death,'' Jack said flatly. ''And that we know about her and Brandon and Hope.''

''Don't y'all think that descending on her might be a bit traumatic?'' Hannah asked.

"I'll contact her," Cord said. He glanced around at his family. "Tell her about Caine. Tell her we'd like to meet them all. Put the ball in her court."

"What if she says no?" Kate finally spoke.

Brett looked at her, willing her to meet his eyes. But she wouldn't. "She won't refuse," he said.

"You don't know that," Kate countered. "You can't possibly know what the future holds."

"I know some things," he countered evenly.

Kate's fine jaw tightened and she looked away again. She was sitting on the arm of the love seat, and her long legs, clad in sheer black nylons, were crossed. All in black, of course. Only it didn't make him think of mourning for her father, it made him think of the black clothing that he'd removed piece by piece from her silken skin their last night in Boston.

She hadn't ignored him then, that's for damn sure.

"While you're doing that, I'm going to head to Tyler," Jake announced abruptly. "Nose around."

Brett noticed that nobody seemed surprised. Of all of them, Jack seemed to be the one most uncomfortable with Caine's death. None of them could pretend to be extremely grief stricken. But Jack…well, he seemed to have an extra layer of something unspoken that the rest of the Stockwells didn't.

"Kate? Would you like me to see that the painting of Brandon and Hope is framed and hung in the hallway with the others?"

Kate stirred at that, looking at Caroline in surprise. "It's not up to me."

"It is your painting," Caroline said. "Who else is it up to if not you?"

"Brett bought the painting," Kate said. "An expense related to the case. It belongs to the family. Not me.

But, yes, I suppose it should be framed and hung, just like the portrait that Jack brought back from France.''

''Actually, it wasn't submitted as an expense,'' Brett admitted, watching Kate. ''I bought it outright.'' Which Caroline knew because she'd been on the phone about another case that his firm had been handling for her legal practice when Maria went ballistic about the money.

''Then you can take it with you when you leave today. Frame it. Don't frame it. Hang it on the wall in your home or leave it in the trunk of your car. It has nothing to do with me.'' Her cheeks suddenly filled with color and she rose, smoothing her palms down her narrow black dress. ''Excuse me.''

She sailed out of the sunroom and Brett suddenly found himself the focus of everyone's attention. He pushed down the lock on his briefcase and grabbed the handle. He had news for Kate about Bobby, but obviously she was in no mood to hear anything from him.

''Speaking of expenses—'' Cord's voice was smooth. ''When you've got the invoice drawn up, send it to my attention here at the house.''

''There won't be any invoice.'' Brett's voice was flat. Which was why Maria, when he'd told her to tear up the invoice, had been ranting and raving loud enough for Caroline to hear on the other end of their brief telephone call. ''Consider it a gift from an old friend. I'd like to tell you that I'm sorry about your father, but I can't. I do wish you good luck with your mother, though.''

Then he walked out of the sunroom and headed straight for the main foyer. He hoped to hell that the mansion turned into a happier place with Caine gone.

He supposed it probably would, considering the burgeoning families of Cord and Rafe.

And Kate…well, if Kate wanted to bury herself in her work and be the doting aunt to her niece and nephew, then it was no business of his.

He went out the front door. His car was parked a ways down the driveway and he headed straight for it. The sooner he got this whole Stockwell thing out of his head, the better.

His briefcase hit the passenger seat with a tad too much force and it sprang open again, spilling its contents across the seat and the floor. Swearing under his breath, he leaned over and began shoveling the files and papers back inside. But when he came to the small leather box that had also tumbled out, he went still.

He sat there, behind the wheel of his car, the hot sun blazing down on him, and flipped open the jeweler's box, staring at the contents.

He had taken a third job to pay for the ring. Working weekends with a landscape contractor. Because even at twenty years old he'd been damned if he'd live his life on credit. It had taken months, but he'd paid for the ring in cash. And it had been worth every bone-grinding minute of hauling dirt and sod and boulders when he'd given the ring to Kate.

God, he'd loved her.

And he cursed Caine to hell and beyond for managing to separate them. And even more, he cursed himself for being stupid enough to let it happen.

He blew out an impatient breath, tossing the ring back into his still-open briefcase. He didn't know why he continued carrying the box around with him. Not after all these years. If Kate knew, she'd probably have one hell of a good laugh over it.

He turned the ignition, feeling the powerful engine leap to life and looked back at the mansion. The mansion where the princess would continue hiding from life, believing that she was half a woman simply because she couldn't bear a child. His gaze instinctively drifted along the house, having no trouble whatsoever in finding the windows of Kate's suite.

He'd slipped through those windows in the dead of night once, just to leave a white rose on the pillow beside her in honor of her seventeenth birthday. She'd awakened when he'd leaned over her and had lifted her arms to him as if it was a completely natural thing to find him sneaking through her room at two in the morning. They'd kissed and she'd rolled over, hugging her pillow to her cheek as she slid back into sleep.

He'd climbed back out the window and gone home to the Orwell estate and the small apartment he shared with his mother near the back of the house. He hadn't slept at all that night.

And now, Brett sat there under the blazing sun and remembered why.

That was the night he'd known that, sooner or later, Katy Stockwell would be his wife.

He glanced again at the tall window. Saw the flicker of the sheer drapes and went still. Waiting.

There. Another flicker. His neck prickled and he slowly reached for the jeweler's case as he turned off the engine and climbed out of the car. He shrugged off the jacket of his dark gray suit and tossed it in the car, along with the tie that had been strangling him since seven that morning.

Then he headed for the house, once more.

And this time, he wasn't leaving until he'd gotten what he'd come for.

Chapter Seventeen

In her upstairs room, from behind the veil of silk sheers, Kate watched Brett suddenly start walking toward the house. She backed away from the window, her heart pounding stupidly.

He'd probably just forgotten something in the house.

She caught her reflection in the mirror and frowned even harder at the circles under her eyes, the pallor of her cheeks. She needed to get back to work, she thought. Needed to concentrate on the life she'd formed for herself.

When she'd checked with her office upon their arrival back home, it had been to nearly a dozen messages from her associates about various cases they wanted her to take on. She'd looked up Bobby's address and left it on Brett's voice mail, impossibly relieved that she hadn't caught him at the office in person. And when she'd hung up, she'd gone over the notes she'd taken on the other possible cases. If she took even half of them on, she would be busy from sunup to sundown, and that could only be a good thing, because then she wouldn't have all this time to pine over Brett Larson.

Pine.

The word circled in her head. "I am *not* pining," she told her reflection. But the woman in the mirror just looked skeptical and Kate turned away. She walked over to her dressing room, kicking off her shoes and tucking them into their place.

She heard a soft thud and frowned. But it didn't come again and she decided she'd imagined it. She slid out of all that funereal black and dumped everything in the laundry basket. Wrapped herself in a thick, white robe and tied it with a jerk.

And then she noticed the neat, pristinely pressed white handkerchiefs, two of them, sitting atop the built-in vanity. Brett's handkerchiefs. She'd never given them back to him.

Her hand trembled as she reached for them. Smoothing her thumb over the soft-crisp surface. She lifted them to her face. Inhaled. And felt an ache too deep for tears inside her because the handkerchiefs smelled only of having been freshly laundered.

Brett's scent was gone.

Her hands tightened around the squares and she moved, blindly, through to her bedroom.

Brett's scent was gone. Brett was gone.

She swallowed and pressed the square to her cheek, wishing that she'd never let them find their way into her laundry.

Then she opened her eyes and saw Brett standing there, the sun gleaming in from behind him. Her fingers went lax and the handkerchiefs fell. She instinctively looked across to her bedroom door. It was closed. Still locked from the inside, just the way she'd left it because she hadn't wanted one single interruption to her pathetic pity party.

And then he took a step forward out of the beam of sunlight. He wasn't a mirage. He was real. And he was here. Her heart jittered. "What are you doing here?"

His eyes were so dark. So deep. And they seemed to see right into her soul. "Bobby Morales's mother was planning to get a divorce," he said.

Whatever half-fantasy that had formed in Kate's mind, it hadn't been this. "How do you know that? None of the family mentioned it to me."

"She hadn't told her husband because she was apparently afraid it would send him on another bender. But she confided in her mother-in-law." He pulled a folded piece of paper from his pocket and handed it to her. "Which was definitely a mistake. Not only do Bobby's grandparents have something against therapy, but they are seriously opposed to divorce."

Kate moistened her lips and reached for the paper, unfolding it. "I know their so-called religion prohibits a lot of things."

"Apparently it doesn't prohibit manslaughter."

Kate looked at the document, gasping. It was a copy of an arrest warrant for Hilde Morales, Bobby's grandmother, dated for the previous day. "Are you serious?"

"After a night in interrogation, she confessed this morning. She forced the sleeping pills down her daughter-in-law, to keep her from divorcing her son. Bobby's father has taken him from Hilde's house where they've all been living like some big happy family and checked into a motel on the outskirts of Grandview. I imagine you'll be hearing from him soon to start working with Bobby again.''

Kate sank on the edge of the bed, hardly able to believe it. ''You did it. In such a short time, you did it. You've saved Bobby.''

''You believed in the boy,'' Brett said. ''The only one who did. I think that makes you responsible for any saving being done.''

Kate carefully folded the warrant on its creases. ''Maybe we did it together.''

''Maybe we did.''

She rose, suddenly restless. ''Why didn't you tell me this earlier today?''

''You were busy ignoring me.''

''I—'' Her denial died. ''I didn't know what to say. After everything that has happened.''

His gaze pinned her in place. ''Do you love me, Kate?''

She blinked. Swayed. ''What?''

''Do you?''

She tried to tell him no. She truly tried. But the lie wouldn't come. ''I've loved you since we were kids.''

''Then marry me.''

Her lips parted. ''What? No! You don't know what you're asking.''

''I know exactly what I'm asking,'' he countered steadily.

Her hands lifted. Fell. ''But I, I c-can't have children. I won't do that to you.''

''*Do* that to me.''

''I won't saddle you with a wife who can't give you what you're going to want!''

''Which is what? A beautiful woman in my heart. In my arms. In my bed. A beautiful woman whose mind challenges me, whose humor delights me? What exactly is it I'm going to want?''

''You're not listening to me at all.''

''Pretty damn frustrating, isn't it?''

''Stop joking! I couldn't bear it to have you walk away from me, Brett. Last time it nearly killed me. I still have nightmares about it.''

He swore softly. ''So that's what they were about.'' He shook his head. ''Last time we were both being deluded by your saint of a father.''

''It doesn't matter anymore. I won't marry you, knowing that someday you're going to look at me and see all the things that I'm not able to give you. Eventually you'd decide I wasn't enough of a wife and you'd find someone else. Someone who could give you a child.''

''I wouldn't do that, Kate.''

''Why not?'' She dashed her fingers over her wet cheeks. ''Hamilton did.''

''I'm not Hamilton Orwell,'' Brett said mildly. ''I want to marry *you*. End of story. If you can't have children, then we don't have children. For God's sake, Kate, did you ever once hear me wax eloquent over the idea of changing diapers?''

''Hamilton said it didn't matter, either.''

''Well, like I said. Hamilton was a blooming idiot.'' Brett kept his temper with an effort. He hated it that she'd married another man, but he'd come to understand a little bit of the why of it. ''And I don't plan on having any mistresses.''

''Neither did he,'' Kate said wearily. ''But it did happen. After we learned about my…problem. And even though I knew I didn't love him like a wife should, it still hurt.''

"Does it occur to you that his outside interest had more to do with *that* than anything else?" Brett pushed her chin up until she had to look at him. "I want you, Kate. Just you. All the rest is something we can deal with. Together."

Her lips trembled. "You'll change your mind. And it will destroy me, Brett."

"So you won't take a chance on the here and now just because of some crazy suspicion you've got about the future? God, Kate. You're not that much of a coward. And you know, we *both* know, that nothing is for certain in this life."

He suddenly tipped her onto the bed, pinning her to it with his weight, whisking the tie of her robe free, parting the fabric to bare her to him.

She gasped. Then jerked and clutched her fingers in his hair when he pressed his mouth to her abdomen. He loved the scent of her. The taste of her creamy skin. He loved her. He lifted his head, his palm flat on her belly. "You are mine, Kate and I am yours. And whatever this life brings to us, it brings it to *us*. Not you and me. But *us*. What if I was the one who couldn't give you children? Would you walk away from us because of it?"

Her face crumpled. "Oh, Brett, no. But—"

"There is no but, Kate." He kissed her belly again. Her legs moved restlessly. "You're mine. I'm yours. It's always been that way. And children or no children doesn't change that. Either you trust in us or you don't."

"You say that now—" Kate's voice strangled in her throat when his lips burned over her hip. And then back to her navel. And lower. She couldn't marry him. It wouldn't be fair to him. But...oh, suddenly, the words wouldn't come and all she could do was hang on to him as he thoroughly destroyed her senses.

And when he came up over her, his mouth claiming hers, Kate's reason fled. She kissed him back, needing him more than her next breath. But he lifted himself from her, pushing himself to his feet.

She stared at him, her disorientation not enough to keep her senses from reveling in the sight of him, hair disheveled from her fingers, shirt half undone over his magnificent chest. "Brett—"

"Do you remember when we were kids? Just friends?"

She swallowed. Jerked her robe together over herself.

He blew out a hard breath and paced across the room, looking rangy and determined. "You talked about your dreams of the future, of the great love you'd one day have. You'd have a big, beautiful wedding where everybody in town would crowd the church to celebrate with you. Do you remember that?"

Her chest ached suddenly. If she'd been asked even one month earlier if she believed that Brett Larson ever thought about her anymore, she'd have answered an unequivocal *no*. And yet, here he was. Standing in her bedroom, looking grim and tender and everything she'd ever loved about him, talking about her girlish dreams as if they were yesterday. "I remember." She sat up.

"And that you wanted kids…kids who'd fill up this house with laughter. Who would slide down the banisters when they weren't supposed to, who would slide across the foyer floor, slamming into the wall like that one dog y'all had way back when?"

Her eyes filled. "Slider. I remember."

His jaw flexed. "And when I asked you how you'd know when you found that man who was going to share all that with you, you told me that you'd just know. That it wouldn't take any great romantic gestures or candlelight and diamonds. Just that 'you'd know.' Do you remember that, Katy?''

Her hands twisted the knotted tie of her robe. ''Yes.''

''And do you remember what I said about the future?''

A tear leaked from the corner of her eye. ''You said you didn't care what kind of wedding you had. And that you thought the world was already full of kids who needed parents willing to take them in and love them.'' She bit her lip, struggling for composure.

''And what else, Katy,'' he asked softly. ''Do you remember what else?''

God, yes, she remembered. She could still smell the hot summer sun of that long ago afternoon when she and Brett had been floating on their backs out on Stockwell Pond, staring up at the clouds overhead and sharing their dreams. ''And you said that all that really mattered to you was having someone lying next to you every night who would share your breath. Who'd laugh with you and love with you and never let each other hurt, alone. Because that's what your father did to your mother. Left her to hurt, alone. And that when you met the woman for you, you'd 'just know.'''

''We can have the biggest damn wedding the state has ever seen, princess. Or we can stand up, just you and me, in front of a minister, and say I do. We can have a dozen kids, Katy, through adoption or foster parenting. Or whatever. Or we can decide that you and I are all we need.''

He stepped closer and she sucked in her breath, letting him pull her to her feet. ''What are you saying?''

He lifted his hand and brushed away the tear that was

burning down her cheek. "I'm saying that we used to
know all that stuff. When we were barely eighteen, we
knew all that. And somewhere along the way, we managed to get off track. But all that stuff, it still stands,
Kate. I know you're hurting about babies that you won't
carry. But, God, Kate, don't hurt alone. Don't hurt without me. All the rest is just so much trappings. You know
it. I *know* you do. You just have to be brave enough to
reach out for it. For me."

He grabbed her hand and pressed it flat against his
chest. Where she could feel his heart beating hard and
fast and strong. "Look at me, Kate. Tell me that you
don't *just know*. I'm not walking away from you, Kate
Stockwell, you stubborn, impossible woman who com-
plicates the hell out of my life. And you can lock your
doors all you want, but I'll find a way in, every single
time. Until I make you see reason. Until I make you
just know."

Her fingers curled against the hard plane of his chest.
"You climbed up to my window, didn't you. Like you
did that night with the rose. For my birthday." Of all
her gifts that year, it was the single rose that Brett had
given her that she'd treasured the most.

"Yeah. And I leaned over you and set the rose right
on that bed that still sits over there and I looked at you,
sleeping and I *just knew*. I'll keep climbing, Katy, as
long as it takes. Until you finally agree to marry me if
only because the neighbors are talking about that crazy
geezer with the bifocals and the cane who keeps climbing up the princess's tower."

She laughed brokenly. "Oh, Brett."

"But I'd really prefer it if you gave in a little earlier
than that. 'Cause you and I, Kate, we've got a lot of
loving to pack into the next fifty, sixty years."

She looked into his face. Into his eyes. And saw herself reflected there. Right there. In his heart. "We've done so many things wrong, Brett."

"Then it's about damned time we do something right," he countered evenly. "We know the best and the worst about each other and still we keep coming back for more. Katy, I know you're afraid. You think I don't have fears, too? You're fine china, sweetheart, and I'm a foam cup. But isn't it better to be afraid together than afraid and alone? The past is the past. It's over and done. And maybe, God willing, it'll make us a little smarter the next time around."

"I keep telling you, Brett. Foam is good," she said faintly. "It keeps things hot. Keeps things cold. Just kind of good, all-purpose stuff."

"That's me." The corner of his lips deepened. "The all-purpose guy. And as a blue-eyed princess has shown me recently, china and foam can work together. Beautifully."

"Oh, Brett."

He kissed her forehead. Her eyes. Her nose and her lips. And then he took a step back. Leaving her swaying.

"We've come so far, Katy," he said quietly. "Just take one more step with me. I promise you. You'll never hurt alone. Not while there is breath in my body left to share with you." He pulled something from his pocket and she went utterly still when he flipped open the cube to reveal the ring.

Her ring. The one from all those years ago. "The nurses," she said huskily. "They took all of my jewelry that night in the hospital after the accident. They said they'd given everything to my father for safekeeping. He gave it back to you, didn't he? That's why you didn't question what he said about me not wanting to see you again. Because he had the ring I'd promised never to remove.''

When Brett had never come to visit her, she'd been unable to bear the thought of asking her father what he'd done with the ring after the nurses entrusted her things to him.

''It doesn't matter what Caine did or said anymore,'' he said. ''What matters is now. You and me. And the future.'' He took the ring, beautiful in its simplicity and purity, from the box and held it up. ''Trust in me this time, Kate. All you have to do is reach out, and I'll be there. Always. But, baby, don't reach if you can't trust. 'Cause I can live without children, princess. But I can't live without your trust.''

''Oh, Brett.'' She looked down at herself. Wearing nothing but a thick white robe. But he was looking at her as if she was the most beautiful thing in the universe. Beautiful. And complete. ''I do trust you.''

She stepped toward him, and it was suddenly the easiest step she'd ever taken. She felt him slide the ring smoothly, surely into place on her ring finger and their fingers curled together. ''I do *just know,*'' she whispered. ''And I will take your name. And I will love with you and laugh with you and breathe with you, and never let you hurt alone.''

And then, finally, when Brett's mouth met hers, Kate knew that, whatever the future held, it would be okay. Because they'd found their way back to each other. Because together, they were whole.

Because they both just knew.

* * * * *

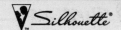

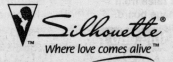

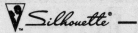

Silhouette® —

where love comes alive—online...

eHARLEQUIN.com

your romantic
books

♥ Shop online! Visit Shop eHarlequin and discover a wide selection of new releases and classic favorites at great discounted prices.

♥ Read our daily and weekly Internet exclusive serials, and participate in our interactive novel in the reading room.

♥ Ever dreamed of being a writer? Enter your chapter for a chance to become a featured author in our Writing Round Robin novel.

your romantic
life

♥ Check out our feature articles on dating, flirting and other important romance topics and get your daily love dose with tips on how to keep the romance alive every day.

your
community

♥ Have a Heart-to-Heart with other members about the latest books and meet your favorite authors.

♥ Discuss your romantic dilemma in the Tales from the Heart message board.

your romantic
escapes

♥ Learn what the stars have in store for you with our daily Passionscopes and weekly Erotiscopes.

♥ Get the latest scoop on your favorite royals in Royal Romance.

SINTA1R

Don't miss the reprisal of
Silhouette Romance's popular miniseries

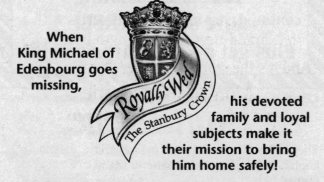

**When
King Michael of
Edenbourg goes
missing,**

Royally Wed
The Stanbury Crown

**his devoted
family and loyal
subjects make it
their mission to bring
him home safely!**

Their search begins March 2001 and continues through June 2001.

On sale March 2001: **THE EXPECTANT PRINCESS**
by bestselling author **Stella Bagwell** (SR #1504)

On sale April 2001: **THE BLACKSHEEP PRINCE'S BRIDE**
by rising star **Martha Shields** (SR #1510)

On sale May 2001: **CODE NAME: PRINCE**
by popular author **Valerie Parv** (SR #1516)

On sale June 2001: **AN OFFICER AND A PRINCESS**
by award-winning author **Carla Cassidy** (SR #1522)

Available at your favorite retail outlet.

Silhouette®
Where love comes alive™

If you enjoyed what you just read,
then we've got an offer you can't resist!

Take 2 bestselling love stories FREE!
Plus get a FREE surprise gift!

Silhouette Books and
award-winning, bestselling author

LINDSAY
M^cKENNA

are proud to present

MORGAN'S MERCENARIES:
IN THE BEGINNING...

These first stories

HEART OF THE WOLF
THE ROGUE
COMMANDO

introduce Morgan Trayhern's *Perseus Team*—
brave men and bold women who travel
the world righting wrongs, saving lives...
and resisting love to their utmost.
They get the mission done—but rarely escape
with their hearts intact!

*Don't miss these exciting stories available in April 2001 —
wherever Silhouette titles are sold.*

Silhouette®
Where love comes alive™

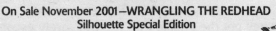